D1104175

SURRENDER, MY LOVE

SURRENDER, MY LOVE

•

Heather S. Webber

AVALON BOOKS
NEW YORK

PRINTED IN THE UNITED STATES OF AMERICA
ON ACID-FREE PAPER
BY HADDON CRAFTSMEN, BLOOMSBURG, PENNSYLVANIA

To Jay, who knows why.

And to

Tommy, J.J., & Jackie,
who motivate me to
be a better person.

All my love.

Acknowledgments

Many, many heartfelt thanks to Shelley Sabga, Hilda Lindner
Knepp, Cathy Liggett, and Laura Bradford for all their patience
and encouragement while reading, and re-reading, this
manuscript.
And thanks to Erin Cartwright and Mira Son for making one of
this writer's dreams come true.

Chapter One

Ohio, 1894

"Everything is gone?" Alex Parker said softly, unbelieving. Her voice sounded taut, stretched to the point of breaking, even to her own ears. "Surely, you're jesting, Mr. Nielson."

The family solicitor shook his head. "I wish I were, Miss Parker."

Alex sat on the sofa, squeezing her fingers so tightly they lost color. How had this happened?

Mr. Nielson twisted his hat in his hands. His old eyes looked wan, tired. "I apologize again. My timing is terrible. However I thought you ought to know as soon as possible."

Terrible timing indeed. She looked at the brass carriage clock adorning the mantel above the fireplace of her father's study. In less than two hours, the funeral services for her father were set to begin. On top of the horrible loss of

her sole remaining parent, she now had to deal with the
reality that she and her sisters were penniless, homeless.

"When your mother took ill," the solicitor said, "your
father tried everything to save her. The doctors, hospitals
and medicines simply exhausted his savings. He's been living on borrowed funds ever since."

Her heart pounded fiercely. She stood, unable to sit still
a moment longer. A loose bone in her often-unused corset
poked her in the soft flesh under her rib cage as she rose.
She welcomed the pain. It distracted her from what was
happening inside the darkly paneled walls of her father's
study.

Crossing the room to the window, she touched her hand
to the frosted pane. The cold seeping through the glass onto
her fingertips was reaffirming—life continued beyond the
boundaries of this room, even though her life was falling
apart.

Outside the window a row of white pines stood guard.
Their branches drooped, heavily burdened with a thin layer
of ice. The brown grass, too, had a fine sheet of ice covering its blades, making them appear knife-sharp, jagged.

Her shoulders shook, her eyes watered. Lifting her chin
defiantly, she dared the tears to fall. Tears were for the
weak, her father had often said, and she didn't want to
disappoint him now.

"I'm very sorry," Mr. Nielson repeated.

How was she going to tell this news to Lou and Jack?
Her sisters depended on her to be the strong one. How
could she tell them that they had to leave the only home
they had ever known? Because if what Mr. Nielson said
was true, she and her sisters would be without a home in
three short weeks with no financial support.

She fingered the small golden heart that dangled from a

chain around her neck for comfort while she searched her mind for another option, another point to argue. However, when she needed to most, she couldn't think of one thing to say. Her world was crumbling around her, and apparently there was nothing she could do to stop it. Hoping he would offer some advice, she focused in on the solicitor. She swallowed a lump in her throat, hating the pity she saw etched into his weathered features.

"What do you suggest we do?" she asked.

He cleared his throat. "Since you are without extended family for support, I advise you . . ." He stopped, a fine blush staining his cheeks.

"You advise what?"

His gaze turned to the floor.

"What?" she said, pleading.

Softly, he said, "I advise you and your sisters to find husbands." He looked up. "The sooner the better."

Alex leaned back against the window for support. The cold seeped through her dress, chilling her shoulders, her back. She smiled, bemused, in shock, really, that he could suggest such a ludicrous idea. "Mr. Nielson, how long have you known my family?" she asked softly.

His satchel clenched tightly between his knees, the solicitor said, "Why, for years, Miss Parker."

She tipped her head. "You've seen us numerous times in our home, at church?"

"Yes, yes I have."

Taking note of the pained expression in the man's eyes, she pressed on. "You've probably heard the gossip?"

"Gossip?" He shifted in his chair as if uncomfortable. "Why, no."

"Come, Mr. Nielson." She smiled. "There's no point in

denying it. *I've* heard the gossip, and I've practically been sequestered in this house for twenty-five years."

"I really don't know—"

She stepped away from the window. "Alex. Jack. Lou. Our names themselves are indicative of my father's eccentricity. As a reformer he raised us to appreciate all life had to offer, not simply what was deemed proper for young women. He taught us archery, astronomy, baseball, arithmetic, self-defense. I, personally, own two dresses only. This one,"—she indicated her mourning dress—"and a night dress. The rest of my clothing consists of trousers and blouses. They are men's fashion in women's colors."

The solicitor's cheeks reddened further, but he said nothing.

"My father was a good man, a wonderful father who passed on to us many valuable qualities, but I'm afraid his teachings have prejudiced our chances of ever finding husbands."

"Miss Parker," Mr. Nielson interrupted. "I'm not sure why you are telling me all this. . . ."

She thought for a moment. Clasping her hands behind her back, she lifted one shoulder in a mock shrug. "I suppose it's because you say our only hope of surviving, of prospering, is to find husbands. But, Mr. Nielson, do you know of any men willing to take on three destitute women?"

"Uh, I, uh—" he stammered. "I'm—"

"Neither do I. Add to that our histories: The gossip. The scandal surrounding my sisters and me . . ." She looked away from his face, afraid that he could see the despair she felt lining her eyes.

Mr. Nielson stood. "Miss Parker, I admit there's been talk of how you and your sisters dress and act, but the talk is nothing new; it's been around for years. However, there's one thing you have neglected to remember."

"What is that?" she asked, her hope stirring.

"Each of you is uniquely beautiful."

Her cheeks heated. "Unique is an interesting choice of words, sir."

"Interesting, but completely honest, I assure you."

Her thoughts swirled. "Even if it were true, could the stains against our reputations be erased by beauty?"

"Men are curious creatures, Miss Parker. Beauty can camouflage a multitude of flaws. You'll have no trouble finding husbands. Mark my words."

"I wish I could believe that, sir. I really do. But I fear that husbands are not very likely. Do you have any other advice?"

Mr. Nielson cleared his throat and bent over his satchel. "There is one item remaining . . . ahh, yes. Here it is." He held aloft a packet of papers. "These are the ownership and insurance papers for your father's sole remaining investment. If properly tended it could bring you much-needed income. It was the one thing your father refused to mortgage."

"What is it?" she asked at once, desperate for anything that might save her family's home.

"Judge Parker's steamboat."

She shook her head, sure she hadn't heard him correctly. "His what?"

Mr. Nielson narrowed his eyes. "You did not know the judge owned a steamboat?"

"No." Her eyebrows furrowed. "I can assure you none of us knew."

He handed her the sheaf of papers. "He purchased the steamer shortly before your mother took ill. It's currently laid up in Percy's Shipyard having repairs done. She, the boat, was christened the *Amazing Grace*."

The air stole from her lungs. Her father owned a steamboat? A boat named for their mother, no less? Had Grace Parker been aware of the purchase? She had to have known . . .

She looked at the papers Mr. Nielson handed her, but she had trouble focusing on the words. She dropped them on her father's desk. "This boat? It isn't mortgaged?" Her voice roughened with raw emotion.

Mr. Nielson returned to his seat. "No. I believe your mother had forbidden him to mortgage it; she knew its importance to him."

The solicitor rested his hands on his lap. "After your mother's death, your father couldn't bear to look at the boat, and had only recently come to a decision regarding operating the steamer. He had plans to deliver his first shipment of goods by the twentieth of February to New Orleans. He had high hopes that the boat would prove profitable."

She pressed her hands together, her gaze never leaving Mr. Nielson's face. "How much is the boat worth?" This boat she knew nothing about could prove to be her family's salvation.

"Your father paid ten thousand a few years back, quite a bargain. He's kept her dry-docked since then, and only just commissioned the repairs on her a few months ago in preparation for his retirement."

"I'm sure the purchase did not help our financial situation," Alex mumbled, angry with herself for the bitterness she heard lacing her words. She clasped her hands together tightly and paced the room. "I'm sorry," she apologized.

She hadn't meant to take her frustrations out on the poor man.

"There are no apologies necessary."

She continued pacing. "If we sold the boat for ten thousand, that wouldn't be enough, would it?"

Mr. Nielson shuffled a few papers, lowered his spectacles. "That depends. Enough to provide for a few years? Yes. Enough to buy back your home and have the life to which you are accustomed? No."

She could barely breathe. This wasn't happening. She simply couldn't believe it. She pressed her hands to her hot cheeks and concentrated on drowning out the emotions and questions swirling in her head. She balled her fists against a wave of self-pity. There were too many questions with no visible answers.

"As a point of interest," Mr. Nielson mentioned, "I have already received one inquiry from a party interested in buying the boat, although I do not know the amount of the offer."

She could take no more. "I need time to think about what has happened, Mr. Nielson. And to discuss it with my sisters." The information was too much. Too much to take in with all that was to happen that day. She could only imagine how Lou and Jack would take this devastating news. Her sisters would, no doubt, be as shocked as she.

Mr. Nielson slipped on his coat, took hold of his satchel and rose to his feet. She led him out of the study.

"You've been handed quite a bit of information. I recommend you sleep on it, Miss Parker, to allow the news a chance to sink in. Also keep in mind my earlier suggestion. I think it is best for all of you." He opened the door to a gust of chill wind. He tipped his hat and walked down the icy walkway.

She quickly closed the door and leaned against it, Mr. Nielson's earlier advice reverberating in her thoughts.

I advise you and your sisters to find husbands. The sooner the better.

The notion filled her with longing. Not for a man, but for a family. To have a baby, her own child . . . The thought alone filled her heart with sadness, because it would never be so. She was afraid that Mr. Nielson was too old to understand the implications of her upbringing.

She and her sisters had always known about the town's gossip regarding them. As young girls they had laughed about it. Older now, they condemned it. But it didn't change the fact that the gossip existed. Thrived, even. In the small town of River Glen, gossip was the favorite pastime.

Even when suitors had been brave enough to call on them, their father turned them away, longing to protect his daughters for as long possible. Now, all three of them were too old for courtship, never mind a last-minute marriage. The idea was simply laughable.

She ran her hand over the spindles along the staircase as she walked up the stairs to her bedroom.

Husbands! Contrary to what Mr. Nielson had said, she simply couldn't believe a man would take on a destitute woman with a poor reputation simply because she was beautiful. And as for herself, she did not even possess that trait to fall back on. Her sisters, yes. They were stunning. But not her.

A husband of her own was simply her fantasy, and not one likely to become reality.

She would figure out a way to save her family from despair, to save her house. As head of the household, it was now *her* duty and hers alone.

From his pocket, Captain Matt Kinkade removed the section of paper he had clipped earlier that morning, an obituary.

> *Tuesday, 15 January, Judge Hiram Parker, suddenly.*
> *Funeral from his late residence 345 Plymouth Street,*
> *River Glen, on Friday, 10:00* A.M. *Interment following*
> *at Spring Grove Cemetery. Friends welcome.*

The carriage Matt rode in jostled, and occasionally, when one of the wheels lost its traction on a patch of ice, slid. His neck ached. He rolled it from side to side trying to keep the muscles loose.

He looked up as the carriage turned down a long narrow drive. Overhead, the branches of the trees lining the gravel lane touched, creating an archway that stretched at least a mile long. Even with the branches bare, he couldn't see his destination and had to wonder why Judge Parker had chosen to have his home so far from the center of town.

As the carriage bumped along, Matt focused on the paper he held. *Friends welcome.* It was foolish to attend the judge's service. He was not a friend, nor an acquaintance. In fact, he didn't even know the man by sight.

Whispered rumors, drunken shouts, voices raised in contempt—this was how he knew of Judge Hiram Parker. The men with whom Matt shared the country's midwest rivers were not shy about vocalizing their opinions. Opinions they considered law. River law. Which was quite different from what was considered law on land.

The contempt the river men held for Hiram Parker had nothing to do with the judge's character. Honorable man or no, Judge Parker had crossed the line with his sudden decision to leave law behind and become a steamboatman.

Though Matt had been docked in St. Louis at the time the judge had bought the steamer, word traveled fast. From steamer to barge to coal flat, word of Judge Parker's purchase spread.

And eventually when the judge, through his solicitor, expressed an interest in learning to pilot his steamboat, inquisitiveness turned to scorn. Then to laughter. The judge was mocked up and down the Mississippi. From port to port, bets were placed on how long it would take him to sink his new toy.

As a boat owner, the men would show Judge Parker the respect due him. However, as a cub, a novice pilot, they would belittle his every move—owner or not. They had continued to laugh at the judge. At his naiveté. At his gall.

But not Matt.

He had admired the judge's tenacity, knowing from experience that when one had his mind set on attaining a goal, nothing could be allowed to stand in the way.

As he looked at the scrap of paper in his hand, a deep sadness settled over him. Hiram Parker wasn't going to have the chance to prove his naysayers wrong—to gain the respect of his new peers. As a large house came into view, Matt balled the paper into a small circle and tucked it into his coat pocket.

The carriage rolled to a stop and shifted as the driver jumped to the ground. Other carriages lined the lane in front of the old rambling Victorian. Horses stamped their feet, and visible white wisps of breath puffed from their noses.

"Cold 'un today," the driver said amiably, opening the door.

Matt slipped on his gloves and stepped down, the gravel driveway crunching beneath his boots. "That it is."

He stood in front of the Parker house as his hired carriage rolled away. He was a fool for coming, yet he couldn't turn away. His plans for the future were tied to the Parkers—to their boat that no longer had a captain.

The front door of the large Victorian was draped in black, the flagstone path leading to its door iced. A three-foot-high picket fence surrounded the yard, separating it from the gravel drive. The naked branches of the shrubs and trees were frozen in time due to the first storm of the season.

He hesitated as he stepped up to the small white gate. When he was very young, he used to dream of houses so fine, tried to imagine living in one. But the squalor of his youth always broke through those dreams, tarnishing them.

Reminding himself that he was no longer that little boy, he took a step forward and pushed open the gate. It creaked, its hinges protesting the cold. The icy flagstones leading up to the house had been sprinkled with sand to prevent falls. Matt took a step onto the front porch, then stopped.

Other mourners passed him, entering the house without a second glance in his direction while indecision paralyzed him.

Through river gossip, Matt learned that the judge had three daughters. What would three women do with a steamboat? It wasn't as if it was going to be of any use to them . . . But could he really impose on them while they grieved for their father, on the day of the man's funeral no less? As the cold wind stung his cheeks, he backed away from the door. He couldn't intrude. It wouldn't be right.

He ground his teeth.

Like a petulant child in search of candy before dinner,

he wanted the judge's steamer, wanted it now. Felt he alone had the right to it since he'd been the only one who believed in the judge. It was entirely possible the daughters would sell the boat in a few months' time anyway; so why shouldn't he be the one to buy it?

Besides, when had he ever done the right thing? He couldn't think of a time. Why then, should he start now?

His emotions warred. He hated to intrude upon Judge Parker's daughters in their time of grief, but if he waited until the next time he was in Cincinnati to approach the family, he took the risk that the boat might be long sold. Sold to William Simson, which wasn't a chance Matt was willing to take.

Resting his arms on the porch railing, he hoped the Parker daughters would understand his urgency and forgive his rudeness. Time was of the essence.

Readjusting his hat on his head, he thought of how to go about making an offer for the boat while intruding as little as possible. After reading the notice of the judge's death, he had sent word to Judge Parker's solicitor. The returned missive stated that Matt needed to speak to Alex Parker. An uncle perhaps? A brother-in-law? Perhaps the judge had a son as well as daughters. It wouldn't be the first time gossip was wrong.

His conscience nagged. He should leave.

Dreams are what we make of them. It was true. If he left, he would be denying himself his dreams, his plans for the future, and he'd worked too hard, and had waited too long, to let it all slip through his fingers now.

His decision made, Matt pushed open the door to the house and stepped inside. Hushed voices carried through air that smelled of wet wool and too many people in close quarters.

He softly closed the door behind him, his gaze seeking. The parlor was to the right, stairs to the left, and a wide wood-paneled hallway straight ahead. All he had to do was take a step toward the parlor where the judge's service was being held. Instead he took a step back.

He had no right to be there. None whatsoever, despite the convincing arguments he'd made to himself outside.

Footsteps on the stairs caught his attention. He drifted farther back into the shadows behind a coat rack near the door.

Then he saw her. One of the judge's daughters. It had to be. Her chin was lifted, her expression determined. She wore a black dress, but not the customary veil that covered grieving women's features. Her face was wide across the cheeks, narrowed delicately at the chin. Her chestnut hair was parted down the middle and pulled back, but several curls had escaped to frame her face, shaping it. The woman wasn't stunning, but beauty was there, lurking behind the shadows under her eyes—a beauty that came from deep within. A beauty he had never seen before.

He watched, intrigued, as she paused at the foot of the stairs. Her chest heaved as she took a deep breath. A small heart hanging around her graceful neck drew his gaze. She fingered it gently as if she received solace from its golden shape.

Something within him stirred. Some feeling long hidden in the misery of his past. He tamped it back into place, not wanting to examine the raw emotion. However, he couldn't stop his gaze from following the woman as she stepped toward the parlor.

Chapter Two

Alex simply refused to look at her father's coffin. She kept her gaze focused on the reverend. He had to be the oldest man she knew. The wrinkles on forehead and cheeks nearly concealed his eyes; his nose was a mere button on his shriveling face. His body seemed to be shrinking inside itself. His hands were gnarled, his back arched. But his voice . . . It was as loud as a lumberjack's. It boomed over the mourners in the front parlor of the house. She suspected that the old man was going deaf and spoke louder as a result. At the rate his voice was rising, she decided, they would all be deaf before the service was through.

She stole a glance at her sister Jack, who was seated beside her. Jack's beautiful blue eyes were closed, her head bowed, her long dark lashes brushing against her fair cheeks. Her dress was dark blue, high collared and uncomfortable looking. It was the only one Jack owned and Alex knew it was the all-encompassing love and respect Jack felt for their father that she wore a dress at all since she despised dresses and all things feminine.

Alex shifted on her seat, still averting her gaze from the casket. Guilt pricked her conscience. She ought to be paying better attention to what was being said, but found she couldn't. She was angry with her father and was ashamed of herself. Why did he have to die? Why now? How could he have left such a mess behind?

Her gaze drifted to his coffin, swept past it. Tears pooled in her eyes. She blinked repeatedly to clear her vision. How could she be so horribly, *horribly* selfish that she couldn't understand her father spending all they had to save her mother?

She shook her head. She *did* understand, respected it even, and was sure she would have done the same had she been in his shoes, but her father's decisions still . . . hurt. Hurt terribly.

Her sadness, grief, anger, and hurt were too tightly wound. She was afraid that the slightest unraveling would be her undoing. She looked away, around the room, at the ceiling, out the windows. Anywhere to occupy her mind.

Finally, her gaze landed on Lou. Where Jack was untamed, Lou was shy. At twenty, she was the youngest and smallest sister, yet her diminutive height did not detract from her wholesome beauty. In fact the opposite was true. It added to it. Lou looked pixie-like, as if she were a fairy. Her hair was a dark blond that possessed streaks of gold. Her milky white skin was smooth and flawless. She was dainty. Doll-like. Where Jack shunned femininity, Lou embraced it—much to their father's dismay.

Lou's mourning dress was of a more recent fashion, with puffed sleeves, a straighter skirt and the fabric trimmed with black lace. She even wore a hat with an attached veil that shadowed her face. But even the shading could not hide Lou's beauty, and knowing Lou as well as Alex did, she was well aware that the beauty which lay beneath the surface of her sister's face was ten times more glowing than what was visible.

Suddenly, snippets of her earlier conversation with Mr. Nielson played through Alex's thoughts.

"Each of you is uniquely beautiful."

How could others, people who barely knew their names, know what she and her sisters were truly like beyond their appearances? How could they know that Lou had a singing voice that could bring the hardest of individuals to their knees? Or that Jack had a mystifying way with animals? How could they know that she herself wrote stories for the children she would never have?

Why would a man want to marry a woman he didn't know these things about? How could he choose a wife based on the shape of her lips or the curve of her hip?

But Alex knew that it was these physical qualities that would find her sisters husbands.

She glanced at Lou and Jack, then looked away. After mulling over her earlier conversation with Mr. Nielson, Alex had reluctantly decided that what was best for her sisters *was* to find them husbands. Mr. Nielson was right; it was the best solution. It wasn't the answer for her no matter how much she secretly longed to be married and raise a family, but Jack and Lou were younger, beautiful. They had a chance at happiness.

Only how to convince the two of them of her plans?

Alex drew her shoulders back, trying to loosen her tense muscles. Her sisters' beauty hid the fact that they were both equally stubborn in their own ways.

Once Alex had the chance to explain the situation, the

foreclosing of the house, the steamboat, perhaps they wouldn't complain about finding husbands. But Alex had the feeling that it wasn't going to be so easy.

Reverend Pierson droned on. Alex blocked out his words and kept her attention focused elsewhere, to evade the inevitable. A few mourners she recognized, most she did not. Being a judge, her father had many far-reaching acquaintances, and it did not surprise her in the least that their large home was filled with people.

However Alex had to bitterly wonder how many people had come with sincere sympathies and how many had come to add fuel to the town's gossip mill. She had no doubt that accounts of what she and her sisters were wearing and how they had behaved would spread like wildfire through River Glen once the service was completed.

Alex's inherent mischief made her want to stand atop her chair and break into song, just to see the reaction generated. The image caused her to smile.

Jack leaned toward her. "What is so funny?" she whispered.

"Nothing." Alex bit her lip. Perhaps she was as much a heathen as townsfolk had long accused. How could she be thinking such thoughts at her father's funeral?

Her father had been the only man who had ever loved her. After Grace Parker had died several years before, her father had become her world. He had been her friend. Her teacher. She had relied on him. She loved him.

And now he was gone.

Her eyes welled.

She shifted in her seat and her handkerchief fell to the ground. As she bent to retrieve it, the loose whalebone of her corset poked her in the ribs. She pressed her lips together to keep from crying out in pain.

"Allow me," a deep voice whispered to her from behind.

Alex tried to place the voice but could not. She would have known if she'd heard it before, for it was deep and rich, a sound she found particularly pleasing. A tingling awareness danced over her skin, causing her heart to beat faster. Heat rose into her cheeks.

A strong masculine hand held her handkerchief to her left side. She grasped the handkerchief, and as she tugged gently, her breath hitched, for above the edge of her black gloves the stranger's finger brushed her wrist. One simple stroke of a rough, callused finger. She was completely un- prepared for the sensation that began in her chest and set- tled in her lower stomach. She was sure Jack could hear her heart thudding against the walls of her chest.

"You're very kind," she whispered over her shoulder, trying to sneak a peek at the man. It was impossible. He sat out of her peripheral view. The only way she would be able to see his face would be to turn completely around, which would not do in the middle of her father's service.

"My pleasure," he replied.

At the sound of his hoarse whisper, her thoughts scat- tered in a dozen different directions. One of which was Mr. Nielson's suggestion: *I advise you and your sisters to find husbands. The sooner the better.* She tried to dismiss the notion, but her thoughts wouldn't obey.

That smooth, deep voice had to belong to a man who was strong, secure, sure of himself—all the qualities she admired and found attractive in a man. He couldn't possibly be married, she decided. The fates wouldn't be so cruel.

Ignoring the strong urge to drop her handkerchief on purpose, she drew her hands together on her lap and rubbed her wrist with the pad of her thumb, amazed that she could still feel his brief touch so acutely. It piqued her curiosity as to how a stranger could cause such an effect on her senses.

Pressing her handkerchief to her lips, she tugged at the high collar of her dress, which seemed to be choking her as perspiration dampened her brow.

"Alex?" Jack said quietly. "Are you well?"

"Fine," she whispered, appalled at her own emotions.

Alex deemed she was in fact a heathen. She was having impure feelings about a stranger at her father's own funeral! She thought about confessing her sins to the reverend but changed her mind. It was bad enough to be thinking the sinful thoughts—she absolutely did not want to shout them to be heard by the reverend. She would atone silently.

Again she tried to look behind her, over her right shoulder this time, but she could not twist far enough due to the confines of the corset. It wasn't often she wore it, but she was determined never to wear it again.

Her gaze landed on the reverend and she kept it there, unwilling to explore the sensations the anonymous man had elicited in her. It simply wasn't the proper time. Later, yes, later, she would explore to her heart's content.

She raised her gaze to the reverend, who was offering a closing prayer. She added her own silent good-bye and prayed that someday she could find it in her heart to forgive her father for leaving her.

When the reverend spoke again, Alex winced, as he shouted the invitation for close friends to attend the interment. People around them stood, their coats bulky, their hats in hand. Alex rose. As she tucked her handkerchief into her cuff, she suddenly remembered the stranger's touch on her wrist . . . how it had made her feel.

Her stomach twisted, her breath quickened.

What would he look like? Was he tall like she? Short?

Dark? Light? Would his eyes be kind? Or would they show no emotion? Would he, she wondered, be a man who could look past her flaws and see her for all she had to offer beyond the physical? Was it possible that she could realize her dreams of a family? Was she a fool for even considering such a notion? Most likely, but she didn't care.

The pace of her heart quickened as she turned.

The seats behind hers were empty. Disappointment filled her. Alex glanced quickly toward the doorway. It was already crowded with people, which made it impossible to tell which was the man who had been sitting behind her. Reluctantly, her gaze fell.

After accepting condolences from many of her father's associates, she, Jack, and Lou followed the mourners out of the parlor. As they reached the foyer, Alex paused, turning back. Other than the undertaker preparing to move the coffin to the hearse, the room was empty.

Where was the man who had retrieved her handkerchief from the floor? The sensations she experienced at his touch were waning now, but her stomach ached with a feeling she could not describe. Who was he? And would she ever know the stranger whose one touch made her, for once in her life, intentionally or not, feel beautiful?

Several hours later, Alex found herself explaining to her sisters why husbands would be beneficial without confessing the true depth of their family's problems. It was not going well.

Lou was seated in a flower-patterned overstuffed chair with her legs drawn up beneath her. "Husbands? How intriguing."

"Don't you mean how unlikely?" Jack said dryly, leaning against the window frame.

Alex paced the sunroom. Usually it was her favorite room and cheered her despite her mood. But today its bright interior and flowery patterns did nothing to improve her countenance. "It is not unlikely."

Jack's blue eyes narrowed. "Have you been living under a rock for the past twenty years, Alex?"

Alex stopped, stared at her sister. "The two of you are beautiful. There shall be no problem finding husbands for the both of you. Mr. Nielson said so himself."

" 'The both of you'?" Lou parroted. "What about you, Alex? Isn't husband-hunting in your future?"

Alex straightened her back stoically, then let her shoulders slump when she found it took too much effort to hold the position. "You can't deny that I'm plain. And old. And much too tall. I'll do fine on my own. Alone."

Any hopes that her sisters would succumb peacefully to her plan of marrying had dissipated. She should have known better. She did know better, she corrected, but she had hoped.

Sunbeams poured in from the bank of windows, lighting Jack's face. "Are you denying that you want a husband? She, who sings lullabies in her sleep?"

As Alex sat on the settee, one of her corset's whalebones poked her in the ribs. She jumped up, smarting from the pain and resumed her pacing.

Had her sisters no idea how lovely they were? She paled in comparison. A dull brown color, her curls refused taming by comb. Her eyes were a duller brown than her hair and not at all remarkable. And she was tall. Taller than all the other girls she knew. She was cursed with her father's height and hated every inch of it.

Jack crossed the room, taking Alex's chin in her hand and lifting it, tsking. Alex knew the dark smudges beneath her eyes were unbecoming, but she had been unable to cover them with her little supply of powder. She seemed to have aged several years in the past few days. She was no longer a girl of twenty-five but an old maid of fifty.

"Such self-pity," Jack tsked again.

Alex tried to pull away, but Jack kept a firm grasp on her chin.

"I admit you could use a bit of powder to hide those dark circles beneath your eyes," she declared, closely examining Alex's face, "but even they don't detract from your beauty."

Alex's eyes filled with tears. She blinked them back. She would *not* cry. "I'm afraid a whole pallet of cosmetics would *not* help me." She sniffed. "And I am *not* self-pitying. I am simply stating fact."

"Hush now," Lou ordered softly. "We will not hear this talk of how unattractive you are. Not today."

Jack said, matter-of-factly, "Your looks may not be the latest fashion. Pale does seem to be the rage these days, and you are anything but pale . . . But, you are a beautiful woman," Jack continued. "You do not need cosmetics. Your beauty is God-given." She smiled. "You're earthy."

"As is a worm," Alex commented dryly.

Exasperated, Jack let go of Alex's face and threw her hands in the air.

Alex sat again, trying to get comfortable. The whalebone in her corset, she determined, was intent to draw blood. Using the tip of her finger, she pushed the bone back into place.

She needed to convince her sisters that husbands were the best option for them. It was the only solution that held promise.

"I'll need a list," she began, "of the qualities you desire in a husband."

Jack's dark hair fell over her shoulder as she spoke. "I do not want a husband. I'm perfectly content living here with the two of you."

Alex swallowed. She didn't want to reveal to her sisters the state of the family's finances. She wanted to protect them, shelter them as their father had done. How had he kept them from learning the truth for so long?

Lou smiled prettily. "A husband sounds wonderful to me, Alex, but as Jack said, unlikely. None of us know how to keep house. Or to cook or sew."

Alex tried to placate. "I'll find you someone wealthy. You'll have servants."

Jack shook her head. "What if the man I want isn't rich? Most of the men I find attractive are gamblers. Ruffians," she added in a tone meant to rile.

Alex jumped up. "You can learn to keep house. We learned to shoot a bow and arrow, for heaven's sake. I think we can learn to bake a pie." She turned to Jack. "And as long as he's a successful gambler, and you love him, you'll have my blessing," she said sweetly, calling her sister's bluff.

Jack's blue eyes narrowed. "What is it you're hiding, Alex?"

Alex pressed her hand to her chest and tried valiantly not to blink. "I'm not hiding a thing."

Lou stood. "What has happened?"

Against her will, her left eyelid fluttered. "I'm hiding nothing." She needed their acceptance of her plans *before* she told them of their family's debt. It would influence their decision to marry. She knew them too well. They would do the honorable thing and allow the burden of their family's trouble to fall on them also. She didn't want to let that happen.

Her fingers smoothed the thick fabric of her dress. It was soft, comforting. "With Father no longer around, marriage appears to be our only salvation."

Jack brushed her hair back with her fingers and said, "This sudden decision to marry us off stems from your meeting with Mr. Nielson this morning, does it not?"

Alex cleared her throat.

"You need to be honest with us." Jack took a step toward the settee. "We either find out now, or we will call upon Mr. Nielson ourselves."

Alex took a deep breath, realizing that she would need to tell them of their family's misfortune. "Sit down. Please. Both of you." Reluctantly, she told her sisters of her conversation with Mr. Nielson: the debt and foreclosure, the steamboat, and his advisement of husbands.

Her news brought the expected reaction. She winced as Lou cried out in shock. "The bank can't do that. This is our home!"

"They can," Alex said gently. "And they are going to."

"So we sell the steamboat and put the money toward the house," Jack said, her fair cheeks tinged with red. "We'll buy back the house."

Alex tried to keep her voice even. After all, she'd had several hours to absorb the news. "That was my first inclination when Mr. Nielson told me of the boat, but unless we receive a very generous offer, it won't be enough. Then what would we do? We don't have any way to support ourselves."

"Fine," Jack snapped, her temper flaring. "We'll take the steamboat profits and rebuild. This house is too big anyhow. Selling the boat will be more than enough to support us."

Alex tucked a stray curl behind her ear. Calmly, she said, "I don't want to rebuild. I want this house, too big or not. This was where we were born, where we grew up, where all our happy memories have taken place." Alex didn't want to let it go, to rebuild. For two generations a Parker had lived in this house and she wasn't about to have that lineage come to a crashing halt with herself.

She leaned forward. "We have two options, I think. The first one being we sell the boat, hoping for an exceedingly generous offer, then bide our time in a hotel till the auction come summer."

"What is the second option, Alex?" Jack asked, her eyes blazing with curiosity.

Alex stood, the hem of her dark dress swirling around her ankles. Her thoughts ran together, jumbling into a resolution which, if one tried to unknot each thought and study it closely, would look foolish.

Finally, she said, "I think we ought to complete Father's contract."

"What!" Jack cried out.

"It will give us income and provide a place for us to live until summer. But beyond that . . ." Alex sighed, unsure how to explain her emotions without sounding crazed. She watched as Lou shifted in her chair and placed her feet on the floor, waiting.

She drew a deep breath. "In all our years we have never left the boundaries of the city. Don't you ever dream of adventure? Of having a new experience? Of seeing new places? Of living?"

Lou dropped her gaze.

"I think we all have had those thoughts at one time or

another, Alex." Jack clasped her hands behind her back. "But this isn't the time to fulfill them. Our finances are in shambles and we are on the verge of losing our family home."

"But, Jack, we *can* fulfill them *while* saving our home and our finances," Alex said, her eyes lighting. "We can make the steamboat work for us. We can complete the contract Mr. Nielson told me about, and we can earn a profit from the boat. Come summer we will sell it and buy back our home."

The light in Jack's blue eyes flared. "We don't know the first thing about steamboats, Alex!"

"Don't you both wonder what Father had been thinking when he bought the boat?" She clasped her hands together and lifted her chin. "Did he feel tied down to his job, us? Did he long for the river's freedom? Did he, like us, have dreams that were left unfulfilled?"

"Your plan is too tidy. It will never work that way," Jack said.

Alex placed her hands on her hips. "We can try!"

"It's a crazy plan," her sister persisted.

"Well, if the people of River Glen are to be believed, we're lunatics anyway," Alex said with a smile.

Lou laughed. "It might be fun."

"It will be hard work." Jack scoffed. "How would we even go about gathering a crew? We have no contacts along the river."

A tingling awareness swept along Alex's skin. With each passing minute, the desire to feel the river's mist on her face and hear the tolling of the steamboat's bells increased. It wasn't likely that she would have a family. In all possibility, she would end up an old maid living with one of her sisters. Just this once, she wanted to do something for herself. When their running of the steamer was through, she would sell the boat and make a bid on the house. Everything would turn out well. She was sure of it.

"We'll find a way to make this work. None of us are quitters. Father raised us to have independent minds. He raised us to be brave and accept challenges." She gestured wildly with her hands, caught up in the moment. "This is a challenge, perhaps the most important one we will ever face. But above that, it may possibly be our only source of livelihood. And the only chance we have to save our home," she added quietly.

"You mentioned," Jack began, "Mr. Nielson said someone has already inquired about purchasing the boat?"

"He did, but had no particulars."

"How did this person know of the boat?" Lou questioned. "Are we the only ones unaware of this purchase?"

Alex opened her mouth, closed it. It was a very good question. Apparently they were last to know of their father's dream.

"Although I like your idea, Alex," Lou said, rising, "it doesn't change the fact that we will have no income once the boat is sold and the house regained. I doubt any profit we garner and invest will be enough to live upon."

Alex bit her lip. She'd wanted this so badly she had convinced herself it could work. But unfortunately, she was afraid Lou was right. Which brought the conversation full circle.

Alex smiled reassuringly. "Husbands. This journey will also afford you both the time to make a decision regarding a husband. Perhaps you will meet someone on the journey and the match will be based on love, not necessity."

Jack turned from staring out the window and faced her, shaking her head. "I refuse to marry before you."

Lou clasped her hands together. "That goes for me also. It's for your own good, Alex."

Alex sighed in frustration. "You know it will be impossible for me to find a man to marry." Suddenly, the memory of the voice belonging to the man who had sat behind her earlier that morning caused Alex to flush.

Releasing a deep breath, she pushed the memories away. There was no point in dwelling on it. It seemed as though her mystery man would remain just that—a mystery.

"You are both being unreasonable," Alex said.

"No more than you," Jack pointed out.

"Lou?"

Regret etched her sister's pale eyes. "I'm sorry, Alex. I couldn't bear the thought of you living alone. Besides, it wouldn't be proper for one of us to marry before the oldest daughter."

"When have we ever done anything proper, Lou?" she asked in exasperation.

"Perhaps we should start," Jack said.

Alex closed her eyes in resignation. Opening them, she said, lying blatantly, her left eye blinking, "Fine. I will look for a husband."

Lou flashed a smile. "Jack and I will compose a list of candidates."

A ball of tension formed in her stomach. "And I will begin one for the two of you."

A bell resonated through the house and Jack and Lou looked at her, surprise etching their features. Alex was just as puzzled. Who would call on them unannounced so soon after their father's burial?

Cora, the family housekeeper, appeared in the archway of the sunroom. "A Mr. Matthew Kinkade is here to see Mr. Alex Parker," she said quietly.

"*Mr.* Alex Parker?" Alex repeated.

"That's what he said, Miss Parker. He's most adamant he speak to Mr. Parker as soon as possible."

"Did he say why?" Jack asked.

Cora shook her head.

"There's only one way to find out." Alex rose from her seat. "Show him to the parlor; I'll be there in a moment."

Looking at her sisters, she said, "Think about operating the steamboat, please. We need to come to a final decision. I'll be right back."

Alex paused in the hall before she entered the parlor. Hidden behind a large velvet drapery, she peeked into the room. Gone were the benches and chairs from that morning's service. The room had returned to its normal decor, looking exactly as it had the day before, as if nothing monumental had taken place in its confines a mere four hours ago.

The man was not seated in one of the armchairs as she had expected, but was up and pacing the room. His coat, which he had neglected to remove, flapped about his legs. He held his hat in one hand. As he walked, he slapped a pair of kid gloves against his thigh. He was deep in thought and did not notice her entrance.

She cleared her throat to indicate her presence.

He stopped pacing and looked at her, his intense gaze roaming from her feet to the top of her head. Never had she been more aware of her height. As he looked, so unabashedly, heat climbed her throat.

She said nothing at his breach of manners. For some reason she could ill define, she did not mind him studying her so.

"I'm sorry to bother you, Miss Parker, on this sad day, but I must speak with Alex Parker. Is he about?"

Alex's gaze widened as she stared at the stranger. His was the voice from that morning's service! As it had earlier, his deep tones sent a rush of pleasure charging through her veins. This was the man who had retrieved her handkerchief from the floor—the man who had caused her to think impure thoughts at her father's funeral service.

Inwardly, Alex smiled. He was decidedly worthy of the thoughts. He was tall, a head taller than she. His thick dark brown hair was combed back. His eyebrows arched and his eyes narrowed at her blatant inspection of him. He took a step closer to her, and she noted that his eyes were the oddest color she had ever seen. A mix between the steel gray of a piece of metal and the striated grays of the sky on a stormy day.

"Miss Parker?"

His voice interrupted her thoughts. She snapped her head back, embarrassed at the direction in which her thoughts had turned. She decided to see the reverend as soon as possible, despite how loudly she would have to shout her sins.

Alex tucked a stray curl behind her ear. "Pardon?" She couldn't for the life of her remember what he had asked.

"Mr. Parker. I need to speak with him."

"You are mistaken . . . Mr. Kinkade, is it?"

He nodded. She tried not to study the man but couldn't look away. He seemed uncomfortable in his suit but not overly so. His face had an edge to it she had never seen before. A hardness, a roughness to which she was unaccustomed. His appearance projected that he was not a man to cross. However, his features—the set of his eyes, his wild, untamed eyebrows, high forehead, long straight nose, and the curve of his dimpled chin—were very pleasing to her eye.

"Of what am I mistaken?"

Again she had to gather her thoughts. The man was going to think she had little in her head save air if she did not stop gazing longingly at him and answer his questions.

"*I* am Alex Parker."

His steel gray gaze settled on her face. For a moment, their eyes locked before she had the grace to look away. Something sparked between them. An awareness. It both frightened and excited her at the same time.

"I, uh, please forgive me," he apologized.

She tried to ignore the effect of his voice on her senses and remember her manners. "Of course. Please sit, Mr. Kinkade."

He sat on the sofa, his large form taking up half its length. She sat opposite him in a high-backed chair, her posture perfect due to the fact that her corset poked into her ribs if she leaned even the slightest bit to the left or right.

"Would you care for a refreshment? Tea? Coffee?"

"No, no thank you." He cleared his throat, then said, "I spoke to a Mr. Nielson. I was under the impression he is the family's solicitor."

"He is."

"Mr. Nielson informed me that I needed to speak to Alex Parker. I assumed, erroneously it seems, that Alex Parker was a man."

"*I* am Alex Parker. Alexandra Parker," she clarified. Smiling, she added, "My father insisted upon masculine nicknames for us girls as a compromise to my mother's refusal to bear him male offspring."

For a moment she thought the man was going to laugh, but he lowered his head instead. When he looked up all traces of humor were gone from his face.

"Once again, I am sorry for your loss, Miss Parker. I knew your father only by reputation. I held him in high regard."

She noticed his long fingers as they drummed his thigh. His energy was palpable. It was as though he simply couldn't sit still, as if he had to be in motion at all times. It taxed her energy simply watching him.

"I am deeply sorry if I have offended you by intimating that you were a man. It is quite obvious you are anything but."

Obvious? she thought. What was so obvious? She did not have time to ponder his statement because he quickly said, "Have I offended you?"

Alex did not like the fact that a perfect stranger could read her so well. She shifted in her seat, instantly regretting the motion as the loose whalebone poked her under her ribcage.

She was certain she was bleeding.

"I am just confused, Mr. Kinkade," she said, hoping to divert attention away from her facial expressions. "Why are you here?"

"Miss Parker, I'm here regarding the *Amazing Grace*."

Her gaze met his. Her thoughts scattered. It took her a moment to place the name. "The steamboat?"

Chapter Three

She sounded shocked. He studied her stricken features. Even the grim set to her mouth did little to deter from her beauty. He could not believe he thought her plain earlier. Hers was an unusual beauty, extraordinary. Her dark brown eyes were bright and expressive—intelligent. There were fine lines around her eyes, her mouth, but they added to her beauty rather than detracted from it. It showed him that she smiled often. And her hair . . . Lord have mercy, he thought, her hair.

The tangled twist of curls was pinned behind her head. He had noticed them that morning when he had sat behind her at her father's service and for an irrational moment had wanted to remove the pins holding the locks in place just to see the tresses tumble down her back. Even as he thought of it now, heat climbed his throat. He silently berated himself for not focusing on the task at hand.

"You had never met my father yet you knew of his boat?" she asked.

"Most of the river men knew of your father and his boat, Miss Parker," he finally answered.

"I don't understand," she said. "How did everyone know?" She broke off into a contemplative silence.

He wanted to reach out and rub her eyebrows, erase the knot they had formed above her luminous eyes. Her questions gnawed at him. It was as if she hadn't known about the steamboat.

He followed the curve of her lower lip with his eyes as she pulled it into her mouth. She was deep in thought and didn't notice the way he stared.

Her silence was unnerving. Too nervous to sit still, he slapped at his thigh with his gloves. Being with her made his every nerve stand on end. And her house made him extremely uncomfortable, as if he were a lone ant at a lavish picnic.

Gone were the benches and chairs set out for the judge's service. The walls had been bare then, the windows' dressings black. But now the room was opulently decorated. Gilded mirrors, oil paintings, and fancy porcelain fixtures covered the walls. Rich, colored fabrics draped the windows, puddling onto the floor.

He did not belong in a house so fine. Or, he thought grimly, in the presence of such a fine young woman.

He'd spent several hours at a nearby restaurant while the interment took place. Attending the judge's service had been one thing, a show of respect. But going to the burial when he did not even know the man crossed boundaries— boundaries even Matt didn't dare step over. So he had bided his time with coffee and rehearsed his offer.

Now he sat, bolstering his nerve to ask Judge Parker's

daughter for the judge's steamboat. He wanted—needed—
to leave, the more quickly, the better. Because the longer
he sat, the more he realized that he didn't want to go.

Matt returned his gaze to Alex Parker and found her
eyeing him with intensity. With his look, she quickly
glanced down, picking at an imaginary piece of lint on her
dress. His breath quickened at what he thought he had seen
in her eyes.

He shook his head. It was impossible. A lady such as
Miss Parker would not look at a common man in that way.
She would find nothing desirable in his oversized body and
large hands. She was a gentlewoman. She would want an
educated man, a man with no calluses on his palms, a man
with a pristine background. A man nothing like himself.

"Mr. Kinkade?"

Raising his gaze to meet hers, he found her brown eyes
questioning and realized she had been speaking to him and
he hadn't been listening, too caught up in his own feelings
and insecurities. He tried in vain to think of her last statement but could not remember anything other than the silk-
iness of the skin on her wrist.

"I'm sorry," he said at last. "I seem to have forgotten
what we've been discussing."

Her eyes softened. "I have been afflicted with the same
ailment, I'm afraid," she admitted.

Miss Parker was full of surprises, from her forthright
manner to her clothing. Personally, he was glad she had
not covered her hair and face with a mourning veil. If she
had he would never have seen how lovely she was. She
was tall, also, a quality which was rare in a woman. Her
head, he deduced, would fit nicely onto his shoulder. He
pictured it, imagined taking a long, fulfilling intake of her

scent. He imagined what her hair would feel like on his cheek—

"Focus," he muttered to himself under his breath.

"Pardon?"

"Miss Parker, the *Amazing Grace*, is it for sale?"

He watched the splay of emotions cross her face and knew something was not right in this situation.

"It could be," she answered.

"Either it is or it isn't, Miss Parker."

She bent forward, then straightened suddenly. It looked as though she were in pain. "It is not as simple as that, Mr. Kinkade."

"I do not see why not," he pressed. "What would three young women need with a steamboat?"

Anger flashed in her eyes. "I would caution that you know nothing of us, Mr. Kinkade. For a while, you did not know I was female."

Put in his place, his temper flared. Feeling inferior, he took a steadying breath to ease his rising anger. "I'm prepared to offer five thousand. Cash. I doubt you will see a better offer."

A look of panic entered her eyes. "Five thousand? No, that will not do. What makes you think we will not get a better offer?"

"Have you noticed the lack of steamers on the waterways as of late, Miss Parker? Steamboating is not a thriving business. It takes courage and bravery to own a steamboat on today's waters."

With a wicked gleam in her eye, she asked, "And are you brave and courageous, Mr. Kinkade?"

Matt didn't know what to think of a woman who so openly spoke her mind. He was not used to it, not used to women of any kind for that matter.

"Or stupid," he added wryly. "I think I possess a little of all those traits."

"I see."

"Ten thousand, then. That's the best I can do."

He watched as she intertwined her fingers, wishing it were his fingers she held so tightly. He berated himself for his foolish, impossible thoughts.

"I wish I could help you, I really do. But I'm afraid I cannot accept your offer."

"I'm sorry to hear that," he murmured, his plans of besting William Simson slipping away. At least he still had his own boat. Simson would never own the *Muddy Waters*. Not if Matt was still drawing breath.

"If you wouldn't mind," she began, then stopped.

"What?"

"You see, oh, this is most embarrassing . . . My sisters and I knew nothing of the *Amazing Grace* until this morning. I would like it, very much, if you would tell me what you know of her, and of my father."

So the boat *had* been a secret to the judge's family. How peculiar. He shouldn't have been surprised, considering that the family was known for its oddity.

Mind your own business, he told himself. He rose. "I really don't know anything. I ought to go." He had nothing to gain from this conversation.

"Please." She rose to meet him eye to eye. "You must know more than we do."

He found himself wanting to appease her. It was an odd sensation, one he had never felt before. Most of his life, he'd done exactly as he wished. He had no one except himself to please, to disappoint. But Alex Parker with her deep brown eyes had changed that in barely a moment's time. Against his better judgment, he sat. "Where would you like me to begin?"

Instead of returning to her high-backed chair, she walked over to the fireplace and used a bellow on the flames. She turned to face him. "At the beginning, I suppose."

He tried not to picture the curve of her long legs beneath her dress, but his imagination got the better of him. In his mind he could see the twist of her ankle, the curve of her calf.

"Mr. Kinkade?"

He had to turn his head, for she was once again sitting across from him in the uncomfortable-looking chair. He was losing his mind.

"I know only what has been passed along the docks. You understand that it is all hearsay?"

She nodded.

"I first heard about the *Amazing Grace* a few years back. Word came down that a judge had bought a steamboat from a seasoned owner who didn't want to sell to a large company. It was rumored that the judge was eventually planning on retiring to the river."

It had been Simson's large company who had tried to buy the boat way back when. Undoubtedly Simson would try again to purchase the boat; his feelings being that it was cheaper to buy and work the boat into the ground than build anew. Since Miss Parker refused to sell to him, the boat would most likely end up in Simson's fleet. He took a deep breath, trying not to think of Simson, the odious little man.

"Please . . . continue."

"Suddenly the talk stopped," he said brusquely. "No one knew what had happened to the judge's plans. The boat was dry-docked and the speculation along the river died down as time passed. About four months ago, though, rumors surfaced that the *Amazing Grace* was having repairs done and was readying for journey. Soon after word came that the judge was looking for an instructor to teach him how to pilot the boat."

"Pilot?"

"He's the man who steers the boat through the river, avoiding snags, sandbars—"

"I do know what a pilot is, Mr. Kinkade," she interrupted. "I don't know why Father would do such a thing without telling us."

"I can't answer that."

"I wasn't expecting you to," she said, her temper clearly rising. She looked down at her hands—once again her fingers were entwined. "I'm sorry," she said more calmly. "I've had a miserable day."

He nodded, not knowing what to say. He decided to press on. "The *Amazing Grace* is a sound boat. She needed a few minor repairs, which I believe your father has already tended to, but other than that she is a fine steamer."

"I hear the excitement in your voice, Mr. Kinkade. It sounds as if you know a lot about steamboats. Earlier you mentioned that all rivermen knew of my father. Are you a riverman, then?"

"I own the steamer *Muddy Waters*. I also captain and pilot her."

"So it's *Captain* Kinkade?"

He nodded.

"Isn't that unusual? To be owner, captain, and pilot?"

"I suppose it is." He knew it was. "I do have another pilot in employ. It is not as if I am chained to the wheel day and night. I enjoy what I do."

"You must. I am truly sorry that I cannot sell the *Amazing Grace* to you."

"I don't understand why not," he said, his tone clipped. Dreams that had been within his grasp were slipping away, like tendrils of smoke caught in a breeze.

She sighed heavily. "It is complicated; there are financial matters to consider."

"Surely you don't need the money. Look at this place," he said, gesturing with his hand. "You're far from the poorhouse."

Suddenly she began laughing, laughing so hard she could not stop. He stared at her, alarmed, as tears of mirth flowed from her eyes. She dabbed them away with a black handkerchief.

"Oh, Captain Kinkade, once again I must caution that you do not know us well at all."

What was that supposed to mean? he wondered. She couldn't be suggesting that they did not have money. He looked again at the room. It held many expensive pieces and it was only one room. He would wager that there was also a music room, a library, a dining room . . . He could go on and on. His anger was intensified by her obvious lack of respect for what she had. When he was young, he had been glad to have a blanket to cover him when he slept in an alleyway.

He stood. "I think I better leave now."

The humor vanished from her eyes. She rose. "I'm really sorry that I could not help you."

"I'm sure you are," he said sarcastically.

She tilted her head to the side, giving him a wonderful view of her neck. "I have made you angry."

He fisted his hands. "My faults are my own."

"What do you mean by that, Captain Kinkade?"

"It means I should be on my way. Thank you for your

hospitality. I offer my condolences on your father's passing."

She held out her hand. He looked at it, knowing he shouldn't touch it, but the temptation was too powerful to deny. He took it, but instead of shaking it he brought it up to his lips. Perhaps it was a foolish thing to do, but he couldn't come away from the house empty-handed. If he couldn't buy the steamboat, at the very least he could take away memories of the taste of her skin.

He kept his gaze on hers, which was quickly darkening. Could it be? he wondered as he slowly let go of her hand. He turned to the door, opening it quickly. It was better not to know what that darkening of her eyes had meant. It was fruitless.

Even if he were the type to settle down—which he most definitely wasn't—he'd never be good enough for her. Lurking beneath the acceptable facade of captain and businessman, he was nothing but a lonely wanderer with a dark past he was determined to keep buried.

As Matt unlatched the gate, he heard a carriage roll up. He paused, wondering who, beside himself, would be rude enough to intrude upon a house of mourning. His eyes narrowed in heated anger as a familiar rotund man stepped from the interior of the carriage. He should have known.

"Simson." Matt tried to take a calming breath but found his anger too powerful to ignore. It had already been riled by Alex Parker. It was of no use to try and control it now. Simson brought out the worst in him.

"Why, if it isn't Captain Kinkade." Simson smiled under his mustache.

Matt detested that mustache. He stepped up to the man, peered down into the man's rounded face.

"Simson."

"Really, now, Captain, what kind of greeting is that? Did your mother teach you no manners?"

Matt's anger clawed up his throat at the mention of his mother. Heat infused his face. He took a step forward, threatening the little man with his stance.

Simson didn't even blink. "I'm so very, truly sorry to hear about your troubles."

"I have no troubles," Matt said tersely.

"No?" Simson stuck out his lower lip in an overstated exaggerated pout. "Hmmm. It seems to me that I heard a rumor—oh, posh. I'm sure it's just a rumor. Nasty little things they are, aren't they?"

He was hiding something. Matt could tell by the evil little gleam in the man's beady black eyes. "What have you heard?" he said evenly, trying to keep his temper in check.

Simson waved his cane. "I'm sure it's nothing."

"If you've done something—"

"So quick to jump to conclusions . . ."

"If you've done something to my boat—"

Simson smoothly cut him off. "You forget to whom you are speaking." Simson's eyes narrowed. "I have the power to ruin you."

"No you don't," Matt returned. "You only think you do."

Simson's lips curved into a smile. He tapped his cheek with a gloved finger. "Hmm, I wonder what has put you in such a rotten mood? I also wonder what was so important that you made a call to a house of mourning? I was not aware that you knew Judge Parker."

Matt held his temper, knowing it would do no good to vent his rage. A muscle along his jaw ticked as he looked at the pompous man who controlled most of the Mississippi's commerce, a man who cared nothing for the beauty and history of steamboats, but used them solely for profit.

"What I am doing here is none of your concern." Matt took a quick glance at the house. A curtain swayed. Had someone been watching from the front room? He squinted against the sun.

"Come, now, Captain Kinkade. Let me try and guess," Simson said mockingly. "Your visit wouldn't have anything to do with a particular steamboat, would it?" He arched a bushy eyebrow.

Matt pinned an unwavering gaze on the vile little man. He would not allow any emotion to show. It was what Simson wanted. He was baiting Matt, wanting to humiliate him. Well, Matt wouldn't allow that to happen. He turned to leave but froze when the curve of Simson's cane caught him around the elbow.

"Let go."

The words were said calmly but even the hard-of-hearing reverend from that morning's service would have been able to pick up the dangerous undertones.

"You seem on edge, m'boy. Care to share why?"

Matt hated the way the man spoke. His words were always marked with distinct mockery, his lips curving as if he were a cat who had just eaten the family's pet fish. It was a trait Matt's fist would have liked to alter—permanently. But he withheld, refusing to stoop to the level on which Simson dwelled.

"I've duties to see to," Matt said, removing the cane.

Simson poked him in the back as he walked away and Matt's temper flared white-hot. He took two long steps toward the man and gathered Simson's coat in tight fists. He hauled Simson up off the ground and spoke directly to his face.

"You push too far, Simson."

Simson tsked, seemingly unaware of how close he was to receiving bodily harm. "I wonder if the Miss Parkers will accept thirty thousand as an offer for their father's little hobby. That is why you came here, isn't it? The steamboat?"

Matt dropped the man and enjoyed seeing Simson stumble. With one last look at the house, Matt turned and walked away.

"One day you will learn," Simson called after him, "that there isn't room enough on the rivers for the both of us."

Simson's chuckles followed Matt as he strode down the gravel drive toward his awaiting carriage. As he climbed into the hired hack, Matt could hear the sound of the bell inside the Parker house as Simson pulled the cords draped in black.

Matt certainly did not have the means to compete with Simson's deep pockets.

It was over. Simson had won again.

For a moment Matt allowed himself to think of Miss Parker's beauty. Her glorious curls, and dark knowing eyes. Taking a deep breath as he climbed into his hired carriage, he regretted that he would never see her again, yet knew it was for the best that he didn't. It was a good thing the *Muddy Waters* was leaving port in the next few hours, because he was afraid he was falling fast for Miss Alex Parker . . . and the landing was bound to be painful.

Chapter Four

Matt eyed the steady stream of people flowing in and out of the Parker house with curiosity. What were they all doing here? Etiquette dictated a certain mourning period with no visitors. Not that he ever followed the rules, but most people did, and it had only been a week since the judge's services.

He grabbed the arm of a fellow walking by. "What's going on here?"

"Auction look-through," the man said, pulling away and heading for his carriage.

An auction? Why? He tread carefully on the steps, not yet cleared of ice, and entered the house. People milled to and from every room, touching, measuring, browsing. His stomach twisted at the violation of privacy.

He took off his hat, ran a hand over his hair. Tucked next to the stairs, one of Miss Parker's sisters stood motionless, her eyes wide as she watched a woman take a painting off the wall to study the frame more closely.

"Miss Parker," Matt said, stepping up to her.

Recognition sparked in her blue eyes. "Captain Kinkade."

He wondered how she knew his name since he'd never formally introduced himself to her. She must have seen his puzzled expression for she said quickly, "I saw you as you were leaving the other day. You're not a form to forget so soon."

He wasn't altogether sure how to take her comment, so he turned in the direction of the parlor, where her gaze had returned.

"My father commissioned that painting for my mother when my sister Jack was born. It was as if he had known Jack would grow to love horses."

Matt wanted to ask what was going on, why they were selling their possessions, but the lost look in her eyes stopped him. He took a moment to watch as the woman holding the painting checked every inch of the image, a fine black stallion in mid-stride. "It's beautiful," he said, not knowing if it was the right thing to say.

Miss Parker stared at him somberly. "Are you here for the auction?" she asked.

He tightened his hold on his hat. "No. No, I'm not."

She arched light eyebrows in question.

"I'm here to see your eldest sister."

"Alex?" She clapped her hands together. "How wonderful."

His gaze widened. What was it with these Parkers and their ability to say whatever was on their minds? "How so?" He hadn't exactly left on friendly terms with her older sister, and thought perhaps, despite her earlier comment on not being able to forget him, she had mistaken him for someone else.

The youngest Parker bit her lip. "I shouldn't say this, but she's rather taken with you."

He gulped. "Me?"

"Please don't tell her I said so."

She looked furtively around in a way that had him suspecting she didn't want to be overheard. It took a liar to know a liar, therefore he knew without a doubt that the delicate Parker standing before him had just lied right to his face. Yet why? What did she have to gain by telling him that her sister was fond of him?

The pixie went on. "She'd die of mortification and possibly consider taking her embarrassment out by maiming someone." She smiled sweetly. "Namely, me. I'm Lou, by the way." She held out her dainty hand.

"My pleasure, Miss Parker."

"Please, I'm Lou."

"Then I'm Matt."

She nodded, then smiled as if he had just passed some sort of test. "Alex is in the back. The last door on the left before the kitchen."

He tipped his head. "Thank you."

"You're welcome."

The wide paneled hallway echoed with footsteps. The beautifully woven runner that had lined the dark oak floor only last week was now missing. He weaved his way in and out of the crowd, making his way down the hall. Just past the music room, a rope cordoned off the area, keeping the crowd from the rear of the house.

Stepping over the rope, his gaze sought the door Lou had indicated. It stood ajar, but no noises were heard within.

He slapped his hat against his leg in indecision. He'd come this far to ask about the *Amazing Grace*. It was too late to back down now.

He nudged the door open and caught sight of Alex Parker, her back to him. He forced himself to admit that his intention of coming here was not only to learn of the boat's fate, but also to see if Alex Parker had truly affected him as deeply as he had thought.

For the past week he'd been unable to get her out of his mind. Her beauty. Her quiet strength. He fell asleep every night, her image in his head, and woke wondering if she thought of him at all.

Why would she? he scoffed. He was plain. Ordinary. A man with a sullied past who really had no right to be thinking of her at all. Yet . . . Lou's voice came back to him. *I shouldn't say this, but she's rather taken with you.*

He stepped into the room, closed the door softly behind him.

She must have heard the click of the latch because she turned inquisitive eyes in his direction. Color rose to her cheeks. A smile lit her face. "Captain Kinkade."

It was as if someone had just taken a sledgehammer to his stomach. With her smile, and her obvious pleasure to see him, the air left his lungs. He fumbled for something to say, but the words got lost somewhere in the knot taking up residence in his chest.

She stayed where she was, still smiling. Heat washed over him, warming his chilled soul. Finally, he managed to smile back.

"I thought I would never see you again." The red deepened in her cheeks. Her smile faltered. "I mean, what a pleasure to see you again." Sadness crept into her dark eyes. "Are you here for the auction?"

He stepped forward, closer to her. The knot tightened in his chest. "No. I did not know of the auction until I arrived."

"Oh." Confusion swept over her features, creasing the corners of her eyes, tugging downward on her lips. "Then why are you here?"

Yes, why? In his gut he knew she had no choice but to sell the *Amazing Grace* to William Simson, but he had wanted to hear her tell him so.

Liar.

He tapped his hat against his leg. He had disguised his real reason for coming behind the excuse of hearing about the *Amazing Grace*. It was time to be honest. With himself, with her. He said, "I came to see you. To see how you are. When I left the other day, I had the uneasy feeling I had somehow . . ."

She took a step nearer to him. "What?"

"Hurt you. I wanted to apologize."

She laughed. "I'm made of strong stock, Mr. Kinkade. Rudeness doesn't faze me. Nevertheless, your apology is accepted."

Strong stock or not, she had seemed so fragile the last time he had seen her. Still did. It was as if she were perched on a towline, afraid to move for fear of falling into an abyss of grief.

She took a deep breath, swept her hands across the leather bindings of books stacked on a large mahogany desk. "My father read them all to us over the years."

"There are some classics there. Dickens, Twain, Austen."

She turned to him, interest blazing in her eyes. "Did your father read to you as well?"

"I never knew my father. He died when I was very young."

Ever so gently, she reached out and touched his hand. The knot in his chest tightened further still, and he feared that it was fast becoming a mess he wouldn't be able to unravel. "I'm so sorry."

"My mother didn't know how to read, but she was a marvelous storyteller." In his head he could hear his mother's thickly accented Irish brogue as it lyrically recited stories created upon a moment's notice.

"I think that's even better than hearing stories from a book."

"You do?"

"I do." She smiled gently, showing him, once again, her inner beauty. "It's not a gift everyone possesses, and she left you with a bounty to share with your children."

He looked down at her hand, so pale against his dark suit, still touching him. She must have seen it too, for she jerked her hand back.

She cleared her throat. "Would you care for some tea or coffee?"

If it would mean being able to spend more time with her, he'd happily drink swill. "I would. Very much."

He followed her from the room and into the kitchen. She stopped abruptly as they stepped through the doorway, a finger poised at her lips. "Do you hear that?" she asked.

He listened, not sure for what. In the stillness he did hear some sort of muffled *something*, but couldn't tell what it was.

Sadness filled her eyes, and automatically he stepped closer to her, protecting her, shielding her. From what, he didn't know. All he knew was that he had to be near her.

The hem of her mourning dress brushed the wooden floor as she stepped closer to the butler's pantry. She pressed her ear against the wood, then tugged on the handle.

A woman he recognized as the housekeeper hovered within the darkness of the small closet. Her peach-toned face was mottled with red blotches, her old eyes bleary from crying. He held his breath, remembering a time when he was young, maybe seven or eight, when he'd come across a young woman in an alley who had been beaten for some blunder made during her job as a scullery maid.

The housekeeper hiccupped and let out a long, sorrowful wail. Miss Parker held out her arms. The housekeeper stepped into them. "Cora, shh now. It's okay."

Matt didn't know how it was possible to feel the way he did about Alex Parker, someone he barely knew. But the emotions were there in his chest, his throat, his stomach, twisting painfully. He just didn't know what to do about them.

"They're touching things. Mrs. Grace's things, Mr. Hiram's things." She hiccupped again. "It's just not right."

"I know." She patted the older woman on the back. "I don't like it either, but it's out of our hands. You know what Mr. Neilson said."

Cora blotted her eyes with the hem of her apron. "I just can't stand it, Miss Alex."

"Go on home, then. We'll be all right here alone."

Cora's eyes widened. "I couldn't."

Matt watched as Miss Parker propelled the older woman toward the back door, removed a coat from a peg and draped it on her shoulders. "You can and you will. These people will be gone in the next hour. Come back then."

Cora sniffled. "You're a dear one, Miss Alex."

"Go."

Miss Parker closed the door and leaned against it. Surprise lit her eyes when she spotted Matt, almost as though she had forgotten he was there.

"Do you always treat your hired help that way?"

Her questioning gaze swept over his face. "What way?"

He was amazed that she didn't see anything extraordinary in her behavior. "As if they're family."

She looked shocked. "Of course they're family. I wouldn't treat them any other way." Her lips turned downward. Her sudden sadness was so palpable he felt it wrap around him like a blanket. "I shall miss them terribly," she said.

He took a step closer to her, feeling the need to comfort her. "Why? Are you leaving?"

She lifted the lid off a nearby canister, peered in, and replaced the cover. "We're moving," she said tightly.

"Without your household staff?"

"Yes." She lifted another lid, looked inside, and moved on to the next canister in line.

He set his hat on the stone countertop. "Why?"

She peered into another jar and he could sense her relief as she eyed the contents.

Distractedly, she said, "Money, of course." She looked toward the modern cast-iron stove with a doubtful expression. She grabbed a pot hanging from a hook on the back wall.

"Is that also," he pried, "the reason for the auction?"

She glanced at him, her curls escaping her tight twist, springing straight into the air around her ears, as she poured water from a pitcher into the pot. "I assure you, Captain Kinkade, the decision was not ours, but the bank's."

It was beginning to make sense to him now. The auction . . . moving . . . leaving the help behind . . . and why she had turned down his offer for the *Amazing Grace* and undoubtedly accepted William Simson's more generous proposal.

"Do you have a place to go?"

She bypassed the stovetop and carried the pot to the hearth and set it on a rack above the dancing flames to boil. "We do. We are fortunate the auction will not take place until we are gone."

He cleared his throat, pushed his hand through his hair. "I'm sorry about the other day, when I spoke of your money. I had no idea—I mean, I didn't suspect that—"

She smiled as she spooned coffee into a silver coffee server. Wistfully, she said, "That I was penniless?"

He cringed as she continued to scoop—she must have put in eight heapings so far. Her sadness prevented him from pressing for answers to questions that nagged him.

Her dark eyes assessed him. "You don't strike me as the type of man who apologizes often."

Never, truth be told. "There's usually no need."

"Yet you've done it twice since you've been here."

He had, hadn't he? What had come over him? Miss Parker walked past him on her way to the hearth and the tangy scent of lemons was left in her wake. Ah, yes. She was what had come over him.

She reached for the pot handle and jumped back with a yelp. He rushed to her side, examined the redness on her palm. Guiding her to the counter, he soaked a hand towel and pressed it onto the swollen flesh.

Face flushed, she said, "I don't know why I didn't realize it would be hot."

Strands of her hair caressed his chin, his neck, as he stood behind her. His stomach felt as though it had tumbled down to his knees.

He'd come seeking answers regarding his sudden feelings toward her and now he had one. He didn't pretend to understand it, and he knew there was absolutely nothing he could do about it.

She looked up at him. Their gazes locked. Nothing was said as each searched the other's eyes. Matt looked into the dark brown depths, seeking answers to why he felt the way he did for her. She didn't pull away.

His pulse hammered in his ear. Blood shot through his veins. He glanced at her lips . . . forced himself to look away or risk doing something very foolish.

He backed away from her.

"Thank you," she murmured, a fine blush staining her cheeks. "I'm fine."

She wrapped her hand around a dry towel and took the pot off the grate in the hearth. She poised it over the coffee server. She cleared her throat, but her voice still cracked as she said, "I thought you would have left the city by now, Captain."

To his amusement and utter horror, she poured the water into the server, tiny black coffee crystals floating to the surface. "I, uh, there's been a slight delay."

"Nothing serious I hope."

Nothing he wanted to worry her with. "No," he lied.

After stirring vigorously, she poured two cups and passed one his way. Hesitantly, he took it and looked into its black depths.

She watched him expectantly. Slowly he raised the cup to his lips, sipped.

Choked.

Horror lined her face. "It's not good?"

He coughed. "Depends," he sputtered.

"On what?"

"Were you trying to poison me?"

"Oh, dear."

He smiled. "You don't come into the kitchen much, do you?"

She grinned, a sweet balm to his burning throat. "Does it show?"

"Just a bit, Miss Parker."

Laying hand on his arm, she said, "This may sound odd, for I barely know you, but I feel . . . I feel connected to you somehow, as if I've known you my whole lifetime." Her dark, dark gaze swept over his face as if she were memorizing every crease, every angle. "I might never see you again, but please know that you'll always have a friend in me."

I might never see you again.

Perhaps that was why he was still here, allowing himself this closeness. He knew there could never be anything between them; therefore it was safe, safe to be who he was without fear of his past.

He hadn't learned the fate of the *Amazing Grace*, but his trip had been well worth it. "Miss Parker, the honor of being your friend is all mine."

Chapter Five

Alex was in a fine mood, dark and self-pitying. It had been two weeks since her father's death. The *Amazing Grace* was now in the water, its staterooms cleaned, the galley readied. However, all her attempts to find a captain and crew for the *Amazing Grace* had failed. No one had answered her ads in the newspaper and no one had come forth of their own free will.

She had but five days left to find a crew before the *Amazing Grace* was due to set sail. It left but one option.

Captain Kinkade.

It was an option her thoughts had lit upon many times during the past week, but something always held her back from seeking his help.

His visit the week before had been a complete surprise and she admitted, only to herself, that she had hated to see him leave. There was something about him, a warmth exuded that made her want to know him better.

When she spoke to him, he truly seemed to listen, to care what she said. And when she had burned her hand . . . His gentleness had been so sweet. It had elicited feelings she never knew lay dormant. It was the first time in her memory that she had ever longed to kiss a man. To be kissed in return. It had taken all her will not to act upon the yearning.

At the time she'd thought she'd never see him again. Friendship had been the most she could offer, and she was grateful he had accepted it readily.

Staring at the ceiling, her nerves set her stomach to rolling. She was going to see him again, despite knowing that her visit would be an imposition of the worst sort.

She had declined his offer to buy the *Amazing Grace*. It was ridiculously rude to seek his help in acquiring a crew for the boat. She wasn't one to flaunt failures in someone's face, but she was out of options. All other routes had failed.

She was still amazed that her sisters had agreed to her plan of operating the *Amazing Grace*. She had convinced them to go and look at the boat, hoping the beautiful steamer would help change their minds. However, it was not the boat's beauty that had brought about their support, but the warning they received from the head of the shipyard that no man would work for a woman.

Raising Jack's defenses had all but guaranteed her agreement to journey to New Orleans. Jack was always one to accept a challenge, and she told Alex that proving the men who refused to work for them wrong would be a pleasure. It seemed Lou was simply waiting for Jack's approval before she gave her own, and the plans were set. Or they had been before they couldn't find *anyone* to work for them.

Jack, Alex admitted, was still angry about Alex's refusal of Mr. Simson's offer of thirty thousand dollars for the

Amazing Grace, but she thought she had finally convinced her sister that the man was evil personified. He had said he was an acquaintance of her father's, but something in his demeanor told her he wasn't telling her the whole truth. His offer for the *Amazing Grace* had been generous— something he himself had mentioned several times as his offers climbed higher and higher and her refusals louder and louder. But Alex hadn't been able to shake the feeling that there was something not right about the man. Her intuition told her not to trust him.

Heat climbed her cheeks as she recalled his anger at her refusal to sell. It had taken a firm grip on a fireplace poker to convince the man to leave the house, but not before he had made a few thinly veiled threats regarding her sisters if she did not accept his offer.

Mr. Simson had reminded her of a fat snake. Slimy and hissing, he had tried to sweet talk her out of the *Amazing Grace*. She had disliked his tone, his mannerisms, even the scent he wore, which was fruity and had remained in the air until an hour after he left. He could not be a friend of her father's. She refused to believe it.

There was no way to relate her short experience with Mr. Simson to Jack without frightening her, so she evaded Jack's questions, which left Jack fuming at the lack of answers she wanted.

Sitting on her bed, Alex looked around her room. Her personal belongings had been packed in trunks and boxes and stacked neatly in the corner, and she knew the picture was repeated in Jack's and Lou's rooms as well.

Cora, their housekeeper, had been let go days before along with all the other household help. There were simply no more funds to sustain their employment, and the sisters

had been left on their own to pack their few personal belongings.

From the fireplace, a fire spit tendrils of warmth into the
air. Alex fell backward, sinking into the soft down of her
mattress. Her thumb rubbed the small golden heart that dangled from a chain around her neck.

She closed her eyes and thought of the day her father
had given her the golden pendant—her sixteenth birthday.
She'd just settled into bed for the night when her father
had come into the room. Without a word, he'd kissed her
head and placed the necklace around her neck. On the way
out the door, he had said, "So that you will always remember that your heart first belonged to me."

Alex rolled, pressing her face into her pillow as the
memories tore at her heart. Her father had always been a
man of few words, but big on sentiment and affection.

The heart grew warm beneath her fingertips. Alex had
slowly come to reconcile with her father's death . . . and
debt. How could she remain angry with him? His debt was
accrued trying to save her mother.

She was ashamed that she had been angry with him at
all. He hadn't meant to leave them in this predicament. But
here they were. And they would just have to make the best
of it.

A soft tap at her door interrupted Alex's thoughts. She
called out a soft "Come in."

Alex sat up as Lou and Jack entered her bedroom. They
wore solemn expressions that had Alex's stomach twisting
into a knot even before she knew what they had to say.

Firelight lit Jack's serious features. Her dark hair
gleamed, falling in a straight sheet down her back. "Any
word at all about a crew?"

"Not today. Perhaps tomorrow's post will bring news," she reassured, even though she had strong doubts herself.

Lou perched on the edge of the bed. "Perhaps it is time to admit defeat."

The fire crackled, sending sparks into the room already filling with tension. "We haven't tried everything. I'm planning to visit Captain Kinkade this afternoon. Perhaps he will help us." Alex tucked her legs beneath her. "He seems an honorable man, one willing to help three damsels in distress."

"Is he now?" Jack said with a hint of something in her voice Alex couldn't quite identify. "We were hoping you would say as much."

A sinking feeling took root in the pit of Alex's stomach.

Jack smiled but her eyes were set with deliberate intent. "Lou and I have come up with a plan of our own that will save our home, procure a crew for the *Amazing Grace*, and assure your future happiness, Alex. It is a plan you must agree to if we are to bring this boat to New Orleans."

A shiver of apprehension slid down Alex's spine. She didn't like the look on Jack's face. Not at all. Her voice shook like a frightened rabbit ensnared in a trap. "What is your plan, dare I ask?"

The bed shifted as Jack leaned forward. "Lou and I have decided that you have been making too many of the decisions. You are too involved with what is going on and therefore cannot see the perfect solution to our problems even though it is plainly clear."

"Plainly clear?" Alex said weakly.

A slow smile spread on Lou's face. "Captain Kinkade is the answer to all our problems."

She didn't like the idea to which Lou was alluding. What

exactly was her sisters' plan? And why did it cause beads of perspiration to form on her brow?

"When you visit Captain Kinkade this afternoon," Jack said lightly, "you will ask—"

"Him to help us find a pilot," Alex interrupted.

"—him to marry you." Jack smiled brightly.

Alex jumped off the bed as if she had sat on a tack. "I will not!"

"If you're not interested in our plan, then Lou and I refuse to go to New Orleans. We wish to sell the boat outright."

Alex stammered. "But, but you can't." Surely they weren't serious. A woman just didn't offer marriage to a man.

"We can. We discussed the matter with Mr. Nielson. He said father left the boat to all three of us equally. Lou and I comprise two-thirds ownership. The majority. What we say goes."

"Why? Why would I ask Captain Kinkade to marry me? There's nothing to gain in such a union!"

Lou's blue eyes sparkled. "We feel there is."

This simply wasn't happening. Alex swallowed hard. How would she ever look Matthew Kinkade in the eye and ask him to marry her? He would think her in need of an asylum.

Jack rose and stoked the fire. "Look, Alex, Lou and I know you don't deem yourself worthy of marriage, but we also know that's untrue. You're worthy. You deserve children of your own."

Her chest hurt. It ached. A powerful pain that seemed to squeeze the air from her lungs. Not because she was afraid to ask the captain to marry her, but because what Jack was saying was true. If nothing else in the world, children were what she longed for.

Jack gestured with the fireplace poker. "To us, the boat means nothing. Even this house we could live without. Keeping it is your dream, Alex. But we could never stand to see you hurt. And denying yourself a husband and a family would do just that."

"I told you I would look for a husband. One day I will. As soon as we're back from New Orleans." Her left eye blinked rapidly.

They stood silent for a moment at a deadlock, the only noise coming from the fire's crackles.

Finally, Jack spoke. "Do you know that when you lie, your left eye twitches? Lou and I knew you were just saying you would look for a husband to appease us."

Alex pressed her hand to her eye. Did she really lie so abysmally? How long had she had this tic? "How did you figure Captain Kinkade into this little scheme?" she asked.

Jack grinned, wide and warm. "Several factors, but mostly it was the scene in the foyer that sparked our awareness."

Scene? What scene?

Jack took hold of Lou's hand and gazed longingly into her eyes before playfully making kissing noises.

Heat burst through Alex's veins. "You were spying!" They had seen the captain kiss her hand. Had they also seen the way she and the captain seemed to be unable to focus when face to face? They must have. They must have been spying the entire time.

She gathered what was left of her pride, and her resolve, and lifted her chin. She pressed on, ignoring their giggles. "The two of you think that my marrying Captain Kinkade will solve all our problems? How? As far as I can see it would only complicate matters. If, and it is a big if, he agreed to marry me, he would know it was simply because I need a captain for the boat. I won't use him."

"You won't have to," Lou said from her perch on the bed. "He'll know."

"I think perhaps you ought to outline this plan of yours for me," Alex said, frustration lacing her words.

"It's simple." Jack clasped her hands together. "You make an agreement with Captain Kinkade. A marriage of convenience."

"What? Are you out of your mind?" Heat clawed her throat. "Besides, a marriage in name only will not get me children."

Lou smiled brightly, her blond hair framing her angelic face. "That's where you come in."

Alex sighed deeply and sat on the bed. "And what, precisely, does that mean?"

"By our calculations," Jack began, "you have just under a month aboard the *Amazing Grace* to convince Captain Kinkade to fall in love with you." She looked at Lou. "*We* can do only so much."

Alex fell backward onto her bed and dragged her pillow over her head. "You two are lunatics. Absolutely insane," she mumbled.

"Do you deny you have feelings for the Captain?"

Tugging the pillow off her face, she looked at her sisters, sighed. "I don't know what it is I feel."

"Do you love him?" Lou asked.

"I don't know anything of love. How would I know?"

"Father often said he felt as though a horse had thrown him the first time he saw Mother. And they were married within the month," Lou said.

"Sometimes you just know," Jack said.

She wished she knew what to call the emotions swirling inside. She ached at the thought of never seeing the captain again. But what did that mean?

For a moment she imagined being married to him, using her parents' marriage as an example. She couldn't deny the excitement the picture produced.

"As much I might want a family," she said, leaving the captain's name out of it, "I don't know if I can ask a man to marry me."

Jack's voice soothed. "Just listen to our plan."

Chapter Six

Matt sat at his desk, nursing his doubts with some well-deserved whiskey. He poured a small amount into a glass and put the bottle back into the desk drawer.

It had been two weeks since he had arrived in Cincinnati and he was still awaiting cargo to bring south, since his original cargo had been "misplaced" the day Simson offered condolences on his "troubles."

He had no doubt Simson stole his cargo before it could arrive, but he had no way of proving it. Sneaky and underhanded, Simson knew how to cover his tracks.

Thankfully, the *Muddy Waters* was safe from Simson's machinations, but there were other boats out there, other men not strong enough to withstand Simson's criminal manipulations—independent boat owners who would undoubtedly succumb to Simson's power, his money, and lose their independence to the monopolizing Simson Packet Company.

In three long strides, Matt crossed the room to feed the wood stove in the corner another log.

He paused at the porthole. The low-burning fire had steamed the stateroom's window, and as he pushed open the small pane of glass, icy pellets stung his face as the earlier cloud cover released its contents.

The somber gray river lapped at the empty landing. The darkened buildings that lined the wharf mocked his presence. Matt hated Cincinnati almost as much as he hated railroads. And almost as much as he hated William Simson. Almost, but not quite. He shut the window, but stood staring blankly at the city.

If the choice were his, he would never dock in this port for the rest of his days. Business dictated choices, however, and he had to follow what was best for the *Muddy Waters*.

Staying in Cincinnati had become a matter of pride. As a businessman he knew he ought to head to the next port, but doing so would be proving that Simson had gotten the better of him.

Matt simply could not allow it.

However, waiting had its difficulties, and he knew his pride could only go so far. He had already cut into his savings to pay his crew's wages. Wharfage was also draining his pockets. If he did not find cargo soon he would have to leave Cincinnati's Public Landing, pride or no.

He raked a hand through his hair. His decision meant he was stuck in a city he hated with nothing to do but wait.

The sooner he could fire up the boilers and back away from this city and its accompanying memories, the better. Cincinnati haunted him. His waking thoughts, his nighttime dreams. It had since he was a small boy, and hadn't stopped, even after he escaped its boundaries at thirteen, though the whispers of murder on the wind followed him to every port.

Turning away from the city in which he was born, he stepped away from the window. Walking over to his bookcase, he stooped down next to the piles of books heaped on the floor, the shelves too full to house them.

Some considered him a learned man. And, he admitted, he *had* garnered a lot of knowledge through his reading. But to him he would always be the filthy beggar child pleading for handouts on Cincinnati's street corners, stealing what he could not beg, and sleeping wherever he could find a spot big enough.

He stood, stretching his long legs, determined to keep his upbringing, or lack thereof, out of his thoughts. He had more urgent matters at hand. He needed cargo. He had called in old favors, cut his fee tremendously, but still nothing. It was as if the merchants knew he was coming, having ready-made excuses as to why their fares were not ready for shipping. A few had even looked scared. It made Matt wonder if Simson was behind his inability to procure a shipment. He wouldn't put scare tactics past the evil little man.

He picked up a pillow, banged a fist into it and threw it back down on the bed. He was a man of action. He liked to move. Waiting was killing him.

If only Alex Parker had sold him the *Amazing Grace*. If he had a new boat to tend, he would not have time to mope about. A second boat would have made him a little more powerful, a little more credible among his peers, a little wealthier and perhaps a bit happier.

Could Matt really blame Miss Parker for not selling? His offer had been low. Too low for a steamboat so fine, but it was all he could comfortably afford. And she, she had needed the money. He could not blame her for trying to provide for her family.

Unfortunately, he had no doubt, the *Amazing Grace* now belonged to William Simson . . . another jewel in his crown. Simson cared only for the bottom line and would not appreciate the boat as Matt would have.

For a brief moment, an image of Alex Parker flashed through his thoughts. Her openness, her honesty, her undeniable charm. She was truly one of a kind, just the type of woman he had always dreamed of.

He tried not to think of her curls, the way they escaped the confines of her pins and twisted about her almost heart-like face. She was a natural beauty. Her bright soul shone through her eyes.

Shaking his head, he picked up his glass, took a long swallow. He would never see her again which was just as well. He did not like to be reminded of things he could not have—for deep down he knew he wanted the woman as much as her boat. He set the empty tumbler on the edge of the desk and told himself, commanded, really, to think of other things besides Alex Parker.

A noise from below caught his attention. He hurried to the window in time to see his clerk and best friend, Cal McQue, jab a finger into William Simson's overextended belly. Fury igniting within Matt, he put on his coat and hurried below decks.

As Cal and Simson became aware of his presence, they quieted. Matt didn't hear what they were arguing about, but could only imagine Cal trying to protect him from Simson's presence.

Matt stepped up behind his friend, laying a hand on his shoulder. "What's going on?" He saw that Cal's eyes had darkened in anger. The green had become a slate color, unbendable and full of danger.

Simson smiled smugly. "I merely wanted to board."

"You're not welcome here," Matt said and saw, out of the corner of his eye, Cal nodding his agreement.

"You do hold a grudge."

Matt narrowed his eyes. It was a look that had sent many a man running, but Simson seemed unaffected by the penetrating gaze. "What do you want, Simson?"

"Not a good host, are you? Very well," Simson said, tapping his cane on the wooden stage. "I have come to see if you have reconsidered my earlier offer to buy this—" He pursed his lips in distaste as he looked around. "—boat."

The man had no conscience. "Never."

Simson fingered his lapel. "Twenty thousand."

Matt's anger grew, heating him. "If you offered me a million I would still say no." Simson was flaunting his failure. If he thought Matt would be swayed by his money he thought wrong. There was no way he would take one cent of Simson's money.

"That's too bad, Captain. I rarely make offers twice, you see."

"I'm flattered," Matt said dryly. He didn't let his gaze flicker. "But the answer is still no." He pinned Simson with a stare that told him he was treading on dangerous ground.

Simson lifted his eyebrows, mocking.

He didn't seem frightened in the least, which bothered Matt. Why was Simson so sure he would get his way? The hair on the back of Matt's neck stood on end. His stomach tightened as he said, "Get off my boat."

William Simson smiled, an evil twisting of thin lips. "As you wish."

Cal turned to Matt as Simson hobbled away. "A repugnant piece of filth."

"He makes me wary." What was he up to? Whatever it was, Matt knew it could be of no good.

"Me, too."

Matt took a deep breath, trying unsuccessfully to calm his nerves. Instinct and past knowledge had him believing Simson a powerful adversary. There was a look, a feral glint in the pupil of Simson's eye that warned Matt to be careful. He did not ignore his instincts.

"Gather some men together. We'll head to Louisville first thing tomorrow and see what work we might find down there."

He met Cal's gaze, saw a flicker of disagreement in his friend's eyes. He obviously thought Matt was giving in too soon. "Don't argue, Cal. We're not going to prosper being tied to a wharf."

"I didn't say a word."

"Did you have to?"

Cal looked down at his clenched fists. "No, I suppose not."

Matt turned toward the main deck, hating its empty space, so barren.

"There are no passenger tickets available, Miss," he heard Cal say. "We're a cargo steamer."

"I'm not here as a passenger, sir."

Matt turned his head swiftly. He knew the voice that spoke those words, had heard it in his dreams often enough in the past two weeks. He narrowed his eyes on the woman dressed in—slacks? He squinted. No, he wasn't mistaken. Alexandra Parker stood on his stage dressed in a long cape that covered a pair of finely tailored slacks.

He blinked once, then twice, as if she was a vision who

would suddenly disappear. A white cloud caused by the cold plumed from his mouth as he exhaled deeply.

"Captain Kinkade, there you are!"

Matt almost smiled at Cal's bewildered expression. Almost. His stomach was too twisted to allow an actual smile to form, but he did see the humor in the situation. He had known Cal for close to six years and not once had a woman ever come to call on him in all that time.

He conjured up some manners. "Miss Parker," he managed to say. "To what do I owe the pleasure?"

He watched as she walked up to the stage to meet him on the main deck. Her cheeks were red with cold and a scarf was tied tightly around her neck. Her long black cape ended at her calf and the cuffs of a pair of black trousers were tucked into a pair of black ankle boots. He still couldn't believe she was wearing pants.

He watched as she wrestled with her thoughts. Her brows furrowed and she bit her lip most enticingly. Fighting the urge to wrap her in his arms, he placed a hand on her back and led her to the stairs.

"You shouldn't have come down to the landing alone, Miss Parker. This is a dangerous area for women with no chaperone."

"I can care for myself, Captain Kinkade. I'm quite skilled in the art of self-defense."

Matt grinned behind her. She was unlike any other high-bred young woman he had met. She had not followed proper etiquette on several occasions and she did not hesitate to speak her mind. And she wore pants. He had to admire a woman who cared less for fashion and more for comfort. "Really? And who taught you these 'skills'?"

"You're mocking me," she said.

He nodded, but didn't apologize. She accepted his silence, and he accepted that she did not answer him. Tall or not, she was just a wisp of a girl. He made a mental note to have one of his men follow her at a discreet distance when she left to assure she made it home safely.

He led her to the pilothouse where she warmed her hands over the wood stove. It was obvious by the knot of her brow and the way she bit her lip that she had something important on her mind, but was having difficulty saying it.

Leaning against the pilot wheel, he watched her as she gracefully held her hands over the fire, her long fingers caressing warmth into her hands. There was nothing he wanted more than to feel those hands on him, touching him, bringing warmth into his cold, lonely life.

Abruptly, he looked away. He had no right to think such things. He had no right to want her at all in any capacity. His past dictated his future and there was no changing that his station in life was far below hers. He berated himself for dwelling on the impossible.

"Why are you here?" His anger at himself and his wantings, his failings, came through in his voice. He bit back an apology. Perhaps it was best if she knew what kind of man he was. She never would have come here if she knew.

She faced him, her complexion still rosy. "I need your help."

He was speechless, her statement throwing him. He hadn't known what she was going to say, but he never would have guessed she had come to ask for his help. What could he possibly have to offer her?

"My sisters and I need a captain and a pilot, a whole crew really, for a trip to New Orleans. We are due to leave in five days' time and we can find no one. I had hoped that maybe you knew of someone . . ." Her wide brown gaze held his, pleading.

It took a moment for her words to sink in. Why would she need a captain and a pilot if she had sold the boat to Simson?

"You didn't sell to Simson?"

A look of disgust crossed her face and his chest tightened. Never had she looked more beautiful to him.

"No."

"I'm glad," he murmured.

Her head snapped up. "You are?"

"He's not a nice man, Miss Parker. You would do well to keep your distance."

He saw her swallow. Twice. She nodded an agreement.

"Captain Kinkade?" Her voice was soft, soothing. "Do you know of anyone?"

"I don't know of too many pilots here in this area. If you travel down to—"

"No," she said, cutting him off, "it would take too long."

"Why the rush?" he asked.

"We have a contract to deliver a shipment to New Orleans. We need to make good on that contract if my sisters and I are to prove we are serious about operating the *Amazing Grace*."

Her words sank in, angering him. "Why on earth did you keep that steamboat? You have no right to be on the water." He'd heard that the *Amazing Grace* was put in the water a little over a week ago, but he had assumed that Simson had commissioned the change. He never dreamed Alex Parker would keep the boat for herself. What was she thinking?

"Says whom?" she asked, her voice rising.

He took a step closer, to get a better look at the fire in her eyes. "Says me and all the other men on the river. Steamboats are no place for a woman. Do you know what is involved with the running of a steamer?"

He saw the flames flicker and die in her eyes and was instantly regretful.

"I'm slowly finding that out, Captain Kinkade."

He was a louse. What right did he have to kill her dreams? The last thing he wanted to do was hurt her, yet he just had with his sharp words. "Perhaps if you place an advertisement in the paper . . ."

"We have. You were our last hope."

He didn't like being anyone's last hope. He pushed his hand through his hair. "I'm sorry. I wish I could help. I just don't know anyone in this area very well. I could make inquiries but it may take days for replies. Most of the old captains and pilots have gone on to farming. They live in the country."

"I understand." She lifted her brown gaze. She opened her mouth to speak and closed it again.

"What is it, Miss Parker? Is there something else?"

Her features softened, her lips curving up shyly. "Call me Alex, please. There's really no need for formality. May I call you Matthew?"

He cleared his throat. "Of course." There had never been a time a woman had called him by his given name, not even his mother whom he could barely remember.

Watching her cross over to look out the window, he wondered what had her acting so seriously. From what he knew of her, she had plenty to say and no caution in saying it. Then why her hesitance?

"There's much commotion down there. It looks like you're preparing to leave," she said.

"We are. We back out tomorrow to look for work in Louisville."

She turned to look at him, a hint of panic in her eyes.

"What is it, Miss P—Alex?"

She cleared her throat. Again her demeanor changed slightly as she lifted her chin. "I have a proposition for you."

Chapter Seven

"This is going to sound insane," she began.

"What will?"

Alex looked down at the men bustling along the decks, checking, securing.

Matthew was leaving.

She couldn't let him go. Not only because she needed his help, but also because just in the short time they had been together, she realized she had feelings for this man. Love? She doubted it. She barely knew him. Desire? It was something she had never experienced firsthand, but she supposed it was possible.

Her body seemed to have a will of its own whenever she was near him.

There was something there, between them. A spark. An awareness that made her blood rush, her heart hammer, her throat tighten. What would it be like to be married to him? she wondered.

The thought caused a slow burn in her stomach that excited and confused her all at once. She pressed her hands to her hot cheeks and continued to look at him.

Dropping her hands, she suddenly noticed how close she had gotten to him. He was less than a foot away. What was it with her? Had she no willpower where this man was concerned? Even as she thought it, she itched to trace the sharp plane of his cheek, to feel the coarse prickle of his stubble beneath her fingertips.

She swallowed hard as she ached to place her head in the crook of his neck and breathe in his scent. She wanted to overload her senses, to take all she could and memorize it all so that she could always keep him in her dreams.

Blinking to clear her thoughts, she finally noticed the way he looked at her. His gray eyes had darkened, deflecting storminess within. To reach out and calm that storm was all she longed for. But she had no right to touch him at all. He was not hers. Not in any way.

Yet, at least.

It was a small comfort.

"What is it, Alex?" he said with such concern that she did reach out and touch him, running the backs of her fingers along his cheeks.

He leaned forward just a bit to meet her touch. The urge to kiss him returned, taking over her senses.

Surely, she couldn't act on it. Could she?

Could she ask him to marry her without even knowing how he kissed? She had the right, didn't she? She wanted to know his kiss. She wanted to feel.

"May I kiss you?" she asked, then gasped as she realized that she had spoken the words aloud. Before she could retract them, however, he pulled her into his arms, the breath stealing from her lungs.

She braced her hands against his chest, not to push away, but to keep from falling down. She tipped her face, met his smoky gaze as he lowered his lips.

What to do? *What do I do?* she asked herself, panicked. All the lessons she'd had in her life and nothing to prepare for this moment. She went with instinct and leaned in, meeting his kiss.

His lips came down on hers with soft force. Alex gasped, his assault on her senses overwhelming her.

Without quite realizing what she was doing, she released her grip on his shirt and brought her arms up around his neck, pressing their bodies closer. She ran her fingers through his hair over and over, trying to memorize its texture, before coming to her senses.

She jumped backward, breaking the connection of their lips. What had she done? Kissing him like that . . . Heat suffused her cheeks. What was he going to think of her? What had she been thinking? Oh, dear Lord.

She stood back, staring at him, her eyes rounded. Her heart beat furiously. She didn't dare try to put more space between them because she feared her legs would crumple beneath her.

"That, Alex, was a mighty proposition," he said softly, smiling.

What did he think of her? Did he think that she kissed every man she barely knew? Oh Lord. And speaking of the Lord, if she hadn't sealed her place in Hades before with her thoughts at her father's funeral, she had certainly done it now.

Get it over with, Alex. Just ask him.

She took a tentative step backward. Her legs held.

"That, er, was not the proposition."

"No?" He took a step closer to her, nudged her chin with

his thumb, and she saw the confusion in his eyes. He smoothed a thumb over the wild eyebrow above his right eye, his humor vanishing. "Then what is the proposition, Alex?"

She hesitated as she fiddled with the toggle on her cape, then spoke, rushing her words. "I know our friendship is a new one, and I don't want to impose upon you to accept . . ."

"Accept what?"

She fidgeted, tying her scarf into knots. "This proposition of mine is more a business deal. A contract of sorts."

"Is there something wrong with your left eye?"

As soon as the words came out of his mouth, she could feel her eye twitching. Perhaps she would see a doctor about this tic of hers . . . either that or start telling the truth.

"I'm fine. Dust," she mumbled.

"A contract between the two of us, you say?"

"Yes."

He leaned against the pilot wheel, affecting a casual stance, but she could see the interest in his eyes.

"What sort of contract do you have in mind?"

She asked herself again why she was there. Her sisters' plan was ludicrous, but in a roundabout way, it made sense. A union between herself and Captain Kinkade would be beneficial to her family. But what about her? What if she failed in wooing him? What if he never fell in love with her? Would a marriage in name only to the captain be of any gain to her?

"Alex?"

She frowned. "Please hold on a moment. I'm thinking."

He smiled again, irritating her further, but focused his attention out the window.

Technically, she'd have a husband. She'd have no children, but she had long resigned herself to that fact. Her family would be cared for. Her sisters would not have to rush into marriage. They could choose men they loved. It was the best solution, no matter how degrading it was. She would do anything for her family. Anything. Even humiliate herself.

"It's more a union than a contract," she clarified.

He turned his attention back to her, his gray eyes alight with curiosity. "Go on."

"Marriage." She winced as she said it, not sure what to expect.

His mouth dropped open. His eyes widened. He simply stared at her as if vegetables had suddenly sprouted from her ears.

She rushed to explain. "A marriage in name only, Matthew. I become your wife, and you get the *Amazing Grace*."

"Explain, Alex," he demanded tersely.

Her stomach knotted at the hardness of his tone. She briefly outlined her family's troubles. When she was nearly finished, she added, "After we buy back the house, you will support my sisters and me by using a portion of the steamboat's profits. The boat will be yours to do with as you see fit. I will live at the house, and not bother you in the least."

His gaze was pure steel. "Just so I understand . . . For my initial offer of ten thousand dollars, I will be buying not only a boat but a wife as well."

She wanted to rebuke his statement, but as she thought about it, what he said held true. "If you want to see it that way."

"What do I get out of this? Sure, the boat, but then I'm saddled with a wife, and I am also expected to support her and her sisters?"

Saddled? Why did that word rankle her nerves? Why did it ignite a sudden anger? "I was under the impression you wanted to buy the *Amazing Grace*. You couldn't afford her before. Now you can."

"By taking you as a wife?" he said, temper coloring his cheeks.

Was that so terribly horrible? She stepped toward him, her hands on her hips. "That's right. Either you like the offer, or you don't. It is what it is."

He shook his head, looked truly regretful. "As much as I'd love to own the *Amazing Grace*, I'm not the marrying kind, and even if I were, it wouldn't be—"

"Be what?" she demanded softly.

He shook his head. "I'm not the marrying kind."

Alex removed her gloves from her pocket. She lifted her chin while fighting the tightening of her throat. She slowly slipped on the gloves. "I see."

He swallowed hard. "Tell me something, Alex. Was that kiss designed to make me accept your offer?"

The anger in his tone cut her to her core. Every nerve in her body ached. It was nearly impossible to swallow. She was a fool. She had believed that he could feel whatever it was between them. That he knew, somehow, that she cared for him on a deeper level. That day in the kitchen . . . Had it been just her imagination? No, she was sure he had felt it, not that she knew what "it" was. She couldn't explain the feeling, the emotion, she could just *feel* it. And she'd foolishly thought he could feel it too. But he didn't. How could he if he could ask her a question like that?

She would not dignify his insult with the truth of her feelings. She drew in a shaky breath. "Good day, Captain Kinkade. I'm sorry to have bothered you."

She turned to walk away and froze as he wrapped his

hand around her upper arm. She couldn't look at him. She couldn't let him see the tears swimming in her eyes.

His voice was rough, weathered. "I'll see what I can do about finding you a pilot, Alex."

She pressed her lips together and nodded, not trusting her voice. Jerking her arm free, she hurried from the pilothouse. Holding tightly onto the guardrail, she ran down three deckings of steps as fast as she could.

Once on the Main Deck, the chill wind blew her cape behind her as she fled. Hot tears streamed down her cheeks as she berated her naivete.

Her boots clicked on the hard cobblestone landing. As soon as she rounded a bend and knew she was out of sight of the boat, she leaned against a wall of a nearby warehouse and slid to the ground.

She buried her face in her arms and sobbed, not caring how weak she was or who might see her. She cried until there were simply no more tears left.

Chapter Eight

The cold wind howled, rattling the house. Alex flipped over in her down bed, while trying to convince herself that everything would work out.

She was failing at the task.

She thought of Lou, probably still up poring over texts of steamboats, and of Jack who had retired long ago, claiming fatigue.

A branch scratched at her window and her fire needed tending, but she didn't have the energy to pull the shutters or stoke the flames. She was feeling sorry for herself after Matthew's rejection and hating herself for it. She was strong. She didn't need him. Not his strength, nor his alluring smile. Or his friendship.

Oh, whom was she fooling?

A loud bell tolled through the house and she sat up, startled. What on earth? Who would be calling at this hour? Alex jumped out of bed and raced down the stairs, knowing a midnight caller would not be bringing felicitous news. She threw open the door and gasped as Matthew leaned awkwardly against the doorframe. A blanket lay draped over his shoulders, covering what appeared to be icy underclothes and nothing else.

His teeth chattered as he spoke. "Simson blew up my boat."

With those words he collapsed into her arms. She cried out and caught him just before he hit the floor. She looked up, in shock, and saw for the first time that there was a man with Matthew. She recognized him from the *Muddy Waters* earlier that day, but she didn't know his name.

"Oh, dear Lord, you're both soaked. You must be freezing," she said as he helped her lift Matthew to his feet. His skin was ice cold.

"We both had to jump in the river. The *Muddy Waters* was afire and we had no other way to escape. It exploded while we were in the water."

She noted the man was wrapped in two blankets. His mouth quivered as he spoke. He strained to carry Matthew into the parlor and she rushed to offer more assistance. She took hold of Matthew's legs, his icy boots hurting her palms. An explosion! He could have been killed.

Lou came running down the stairs, the robe to her dressing gown flapping. "What happened? Is that . . . is that Captain Kinkade?"

"Lou," she ordered, "show this man to the water closet, run a hot bath for him, and then come back and help me with Captain Kinkade."

Alex saw her sister's eyes widen, but she said nothing as she led Matthew's stiff-legged friend away.

"Matthew," Alex whispered close to his ear, "wake up." She slapped at his face gently. Lifting his head onto her lap, she tried to rub some warmth into his face using the hem of her nightgown. "Please," she begged.

When she moved her hand, she noticed it was covered in red. Blood. Matthew's blood. "Dear Lord," she cried, stretching herself to see the back of his head. A large gash streaked across the back of his skull. "Oh no, oh no," she chanted.

She heard footsteps as Lou returned. "What happened?" she asked.

"There was an explosion on his steamboat," Alex explained quickly. "He and his friend had to jump in the river to escape the flames, and apparently the captain was hit with debris," she said, holding up her hand, showing Lou the blood.

"We need to take his clothes off," Lou murmured. "They're keeping him chilled."

Alex nodded, having been thinking the same thing herself.

"Since I know how you are about blood, Alex, I'll do the stitching," she offered. Her fair coloring reddened. "I'll leave you to tend to his clothing."

Alex swallowed, stared at her sister.

"It must be done."

"I—I know. It's just—" She had never seen a naked man before.

"I know. It will be okay. I'll set some water to boiling."

Lou hurried from the room and Alex dropped to her knees to pry icy boots from Matthew's feet. She needed to get him warm. She concentrated on that fact and not on the bare skin beneath the clothing.

Lou returned a moment later. "I went to rouse Jack, but she isn't here. Her bed hasn't been slept in."

Alex was going to strangle her sister. Of all nights, she

had to choose this one to pull a disappearing act. Usually she didn't worry about Jack's little expeditions to the gaming hall, but with Simson's less than veiled threats, she was uneasy.

"I'll be right back; the water must be boiling by now." Lou closed the drapes to the parlor as she stepped out.

Alex bent over Matthew, willing him to wake up. She unbuttoned his long underwear and pulled the icy material away from his skin, letting it fall around his waist. She tried not to look at him as a man, but as a patient; however, she couldn't help but notice his broad chest had turned a deathly shade of blue. She held her hands in front of the fire and then rubbed them across his chest.

"Come on, Matthew, wake up," she urged to no avail.

Taking a deep breath, she slipped his long underwear over his hips and down his legs, keeping her eyes closed tightly all the while. If he was naked beneath the icy clothing she didn't want to know. She averted her gaze and reached for the throw blanket atop the chair. She put it over him went about her job of massaging warmth into his limbs.

A soft tap on the wall startled her. She turned as Lou entered with the sewing supplies, a pot of boiling water and their father's shaving gear. She probed his wound with deft fingers, then dipped the needle in the boiling water, holding it there for a minute. "Alex, pull his hair away from the wound as much as possible."

Alex's hands shook as she did what her sister told her to do.

Lou looked up at her. "He'll be okay, Alex."

Alex nodded stiffly, but said nothing.

After dipping the judge's razor into the water, Lou gently

shaved the hair away from Matthew's wound as carefully as possible.

Alex passed over the needle and Lou threaded it with fine silk.

"Why do you think Captain Kinkade came here, Alex? Surely shelter was provided closer to the Public Landing. Why would he come here, in this weather, to our house, if he didn't care for you? He must have some feelings for you, despite his refusal to marry you."

Alex smoothed the hair away from Matthew's forehead, wanting to believe what Lou said was true, but knowing it wasn't, not after the way he accused her of manipulating him.

Dipping a small cloth into the hot water, she pressed it against his face. "I don't know," she finally said. "I guess he knew he could come here when in need."

She wiped the cloth down his neck, remembering the heat of his flesh beneath her fingers when she'd touched him that afternoon. She'd do anything to feel that heat again, to take away the chill of his skin.

"He certainly is a handsome man."

"The most handsome I have ever seen." Alex colored. "Oh."

Lou grinned. "You do like him."

"How I feel isn't important. He doesn't like me. Not enough to marry me, not even in name only."

With sure fingers, Lou continued sewing. "Perhaps he doesn't want a woman who won't share his bed?"

Matthew moaned and nodded, but his eyes remained closed and he showed no other signs of waking up. Lou's eyes brightened under her pale lashes.

Alex's cheeks heated. "He's delusional," she said.

"Maybe he was deeply offended that you didn't want a real marriage."

"Nonsense, LouEllen!" Was it possible? "Captain Kinkade made it quite clear he wasn't going to marry anyone."

She shook her head. "His actions tonight tell me otherwise."

"Stop it," Alex commanded. "He's ill. I'm terrified he will not make it through the night. This is no time to torture me."

"Okay, but when he is well . . ."

"Fair enough."

They both snapped their heads up as the front door slammed. Jack came rushing into the room, tossing her cowboy hat onto the settee. "Oh my, it's true!"

"Jack, calm down. What's true?"

"Mrs. Farrell called Mrs. Weiss who sent her oldest boy to the gaming hall to tell her husband the news."

Alex's thought spun. "Why were you at the gaming hall—again—when you know it is off-limits to women? And to tell what?"

Jack grinned and said slyly, "They didn't know I was a woman, and apparently two disreputable-looking men in a carriage stopped at Mrs. Farrell's inn for directions to our house."

"Jack!" Alex cried. "You know how we feel about you masquerading as a man to gamble. It must stop."

"Why?"

Alex's head pounded. She couldn't deal with her sister's love of poker at that minute. She had more important things to attend.

Jack smiled and said, "Speculation is high that we've turned this place into a house of ill repute. And I'd have to agree seeing as how there's a naked man lying on the floor."

Alex rolled her eyes. "Only in River Glen, and he's not naked. He's wearing a blanket."

Jack leaned forward. "Is that Captain Kinkade? He looks different when he's not kissing your hand."

Alex stood, wiping her hands on her robe, ignoring her sister's teasing tone, and explained what had happened.

Remarkably, Jack did not comment on Alex's flustered manner, or her blush as she looked at Matthew. Instead she offered to get the towels to warm the man.

"Wait, Jack!" Alex gasped as she disappeared, heading for the water closet, but Jack didn't hear her.

"What's the matter?" Lou looked up as she tied off a knot and snipped the ends of the thread.

Alex grimaced. "There is the small matter of the bathtub being occupied."

Lou let out a laugh. "Serves her right for going to the gaming hall in the first place."

Alex stood and stirred the wood logs on the grate with the iron poker. Lou had gone off to make tea and Jack was still, inexplicably, in the water closet.

Alex didn't have time to speculate on the reason why, though, because her thoughts were focused on Matthew.

Simson blew up my boat. Unfortunately, her limited time with Mr. Simson had shown her what kind of man he was. She didn't doubt for an instant that what Matthew said was true. But why?

She loosened the collar of her dressing gown. The heat in the parlor was oppressive. Beyond the large rectangular window, winter rested in the night, but here inside the house, it felt as if a boiler room had just exploded. The fire roared, the wood crackled and every once in a while emitted soft hissing sounds and orange sparks. Using a handkerchief, she mopped her dampening brow as she knelt down next to Matthew on the floor.

Why wasn't he waking? His color was returning slowly but surely. His fingers, toes, nose, and ears had already turned a healthy pink.

She ran her hand over his face, enjoying the feel of his skin on hers. The touch wasn't one a nurse would give her patient. It went beyond comfort. It went to a place she never imagined she'd experience. She cared for Captain Matthew Kinkade. Cared for him deeply. Why, she did not know. His rejection still stung. She tried not to think of the way he had accused her of using her kiss as some sort of manipulative tool.

Gently, she continued rubbing, refusing to put a name to the ache she felt. He was more handsome than any man she had ever seen—even with his pale pallor and missing patch of hair.

She allowed herself to run her fingers through his hair as she had done in the pilothouse. Blushing, she allowed herself to remember the last time they were together.

Where were her senses when she decided to kiss him? Her self-control? She hadn't been prepared for her reaction to the kiss. It had rocked her steely core, shattered her reserve. His caresses had made every nerve ending she possessed come alive. It was as if they had been resting, waiting for his touch. Even now, they were at attention, waiting. Knowing he was near. So close, she thought, but never farther away.

A pan clattered in the kitchen. She looked to the parlor's arch. Listening carefully, she heard only the ticking of the clock and the fire's crackle. Nothing more from the kitchen.

Nothing from the water closet.

What *was* Jack doing in there? Knowing her sister, she was probably quizzing Matthew's friend on the particulars of the explosion. Hopefully, she was being tactful and demure. The poor man was undoubtedly wondering who would be so bold as to intrude on a man's bath.

Beneath her stroking hand, Matthew murmured and shifted as if he were uncomfortable. She bent over him, her face mere inches from his. Her hair fell in a rippling wave over her shoulder and rested upon his chest.

His eyes were closed, but his mouth moved as if he were having a conversation in his dreams. No sound came from his lips, though, and Alex felt oddly left out. She wanted to be in his dreams. She wanted to be in his life. It shocked her, admitting it. For some inexplicable reason she was drawn to this man. This man who for all intents and purposes was hard, jaded. But a man whom, she knew, retrieved handkerchiefs, kissed hands, and listened with his heart. She shook her head. Would she ever really know who he was?

"Matthew," she said softly, shaking him gently.

He murmured and she thought she heard "Muddy" in the soft expulsion from his lips. Her heart broke for him and his loss.

Shaking her head in sadness, she focused her attention on Matthew's still form. Her hair that rested on his chest swayed from side to side with the movement of her head, and she was surprised when he reached up and brushed it away as if it tickled.

"Matthew, wake up," she ordered softly.

His eyes blinked open. They were faraway . . . distant. The gray looked ice blue in the firelight and Alex could see the flames' dancing reflection in the pale orbs. He blinked. The distant look faded as he tried to focus in on her face. His lips parted as if he was going to say something, then closed again. She stared at them, remembering their taste, their feel, and she longed to experience his kiss once again.

She didn't feel his hand rise, only knew he had moved it because it was suddenly in her hair—wrapping strands around his fist. The tugging felt so good, so possessive. As if he had a right to hold her hair in his hands, as if he had done it a thousand times.

"Matth—"

Her words were cut off by his lips. He had lifted his head, kissing her softly at first, as if she might vanish, then more forcefully.

If she had allowed herself to think about it, she might have found the resolve to back away. So she didn't allow herself to think. Only to feel. To take what was being offered.

The kiss felt so incredible, it must surely be sinful, but she didn't care. In his arms, she forgot everything she knew she should remember as to why this was wrong. And she completely forgot about his rejection of her. Of his accusations. She forgot it all as she reveled in his touch, his lips, his feel.

"Alexandra Parker!"

Alex snapped her head back, suddenly ending the kiss. Matthew's head thumped to the floor, and he moaned. She was too distraught to see to his needs, though, as she looked, stricken, at Jack.

Lou stormed into the room. "What? What happened?"

"Alex was taking advantage of our patient. She kissed him."

Lou's mouth opened in a silent O, her blue eyes wide.

"It wasn't . . . I didn't . . ." Alex fumbled for an explanation.

As Lou checked the wound on his head, Matthew blinked at them lazily. "I was dreaming," he murmured. "I was dreaming." His eyes fluttered closed.

After making sure Matthew was asleep once again, Alex looked pointedly at her sister and said, "And what about you, Jack? Did you have trouble finding the towels?"

Jack blushed. It was such a rare occurrence that Alex went suddenly still.

"I do seem to have forgotten the reason for my foray into the water closet, haven't I? I was so shocked by the appearance of a man in the tub that it completely went out of my mind, especially since I happened to recognize the man." She sat on the settee. "So what could I do but introduce myself?"

"Yes, what?" Lou murmured, adding another bandage to Matthew's head.

Jack shot her an annoyed glance.

"How do you know of him, Jack?" Alex asked. "Or do I not want to know?"

"Mr. McQue is a gambler. I've seen him at the Maybury," Jack said, referring to a popular men's gambling club. "Oh, he doesn't recognize me, because I was dressed as a boy—"

Suddenly, from the floor, Alex heard a loud snort. She glanced down at Matthew, who was holding his head, blinking his eyes, and looking at her through disbelieving eyes as though she were a ghost. His words came out in between low chuckles. "I've died, haven't I? Because none of this can possibly be real. A sensual angel, a woman dressing as a boy . . . Yes, surely, I'm dead."

Chapter Nine

"**S**top grinning."

"I can't help it." Cal fell back on his pillow. They were in the guest room, settled in for the night by Lou Parker, who played the role of Mother Hen quite well.

Matt ran his hand over his head, feeling the sutures, and more than that—the bald spot surrounding the thin threads of silk.

"You can hardly see it."

"You never could lie well, McQue."

"Okay, you look . . . You look like a circus clown. But it was necessary."

Matt's head ached. Not an ache that was a too-much-to-drink ache. No, this was an all-out, his-brain-had-declared-war ache.

"All the time we were traveling to this small town I wondered why you were pushing yourself . . ."

"I'd stop if I were you," Matt warned, pushing his fingers

into his temples. He didn't want to think of his motivations for coming here, to Alex. It was bad enough that he was here, indebted at her gracious hospitality, and ashamed of the way he had treated her earlier.

He'd hurt her terribly with his accusation of manipulation, as he knew it would. As much as he would have loved to accept her offer of marriage, it would have been impossible. He needed her to see the kind of man he was, the hardened man with the sinful past, so he'd purposely sent her running, banishing her from his life and his dreams forever.

Cal continued on, undeterred. "I think I would have *walked* ten miles to receive this kind of care."

"You're pushing it, Cal."

Or so he'd thought he had banished her. He hadn't counted on the pain he felt at the thought of never seeing her again.

Then he'd gone and kissed her tonight. How was he going to explain that?

At first he thought their kiss a dream, but the unsure looks she gave him under those long lashes of hers told him otherwise. Also, since he had awoken fully, he'd seen neither hide nor hair of her. She was avoiding him, and he sincerely couldn't blame her. She must think him totally unrefined and brutish.

Oh, but she had tasted so sweet, and her hair felt so soft. Yes, he was ashamed of his actions, but he didn't regret them for an instant. In fact, given the opportunity to do it again, he would without hesitation. Which was another reason why he couldn't marry her. She needed—deserved—a gentleman. Why the thought of another man touching her intimately had his jaw locked and his teeth clenched he couldn't fathom.

Forcing himself to relax, he looked at the clock standing righteously in the corner. Five A.M. White gauzy curtains covered the steamed windows, but despite the impediments, he could tell it was still and black as pitch outside.

He briefly wondered if the fire aboard the *Muddy Waters* had gone out. Had her remains sunk? Memories of the all-consuming fire rushed through his head. The frantic search for crew about the *Muddy Waters*, the thunderous rumble of the boilers exploding, and the sightless leap into the frigid Ohio with Cal. His life's work was gone. Poof! Just like that. He shook his head. The thoughts were too painful.

"Why didn't you tell me about her?"

He fought the urge to smother Cal and his inquisitiveness with his pillow. "What's to tell?" He pulled the blankets up to his chest and rolled, trying to get comfortable.

" 'What's to tell?' " Cal mocked. "Sure as I'm lying here, there's *something* going on between the two of you."

In hopes that darkness would quiet Cal, Matt reached over and dimmed the gaslight, the sleeve to his shirt flapping against his arm. He was no small man. He was tall and had his fair share of hard-earned muscle. Even so, he felt like a young lad in the judge's clothing Lou had brought for him to wear, as though he were a little boy playing dress-up. The image brought along a pinch of pain. It was so slight, he could have thought he imagined it. But knew he hadn't. He would never have a little boy trying on his coats, walking around in his oversized shoes.

"I'm not blind," he added when Matt said nothing. "I see the looks that pass between the two of you. Saw them on the wharf, too, but thought I imagined it. It looked suspiciously like mooning."

Matt pumped his fist into his pillow. "I do not moon."

"Could have fooled me."

Lifting his hand, Matt rubbed the shaved patch over his left ear. "This is not up for discussion."

"Aye, aye," Cal mocked, the words sharply reminding Matt that he was a captain. Or had been.

He didn't want to think of the boat. His dreams. His future. Now he had nothing at all, not even his pride after he had practically crawled here and collapsed at Alex's feet. Why *had* he done that? What had possessed him?

Unfortunately, he knew the answers to those questions. He needed her, needed what she had offered him. No, not the marriage. The emotion. The emotion he had seen in her eyes and felt in her kiss.

It had been his first instinct to come to her after the explosion. Somehow he knew she would welcome him in without a second glance, and would care for him, not that he deserved her tending. But he would make it up to her. Somehow, he silently vowed, he would. How, though?

As the fireplace crackled, he tightened his grip on his covers. He wanted to vent his frustration—frustration born from his situation with Alex to the loss of his boat and his feelings of inadequacy.

With the explosion of his steamboat, his dreams, he thought sullenly, were now driftwood. He'd risen from nothing once before; he could do it again, he reminded himself. Doubts wiggled their way into his resolve, though, the longer he thought about starting over. He was older now, the market was tighter. Could he find a way back in?

The pounding of his head returned full force, reminding him of the sleep he'd missed. The low fire dimly lit the room and crackled a soothing lullaby. His eyes drifted closed and immediately he thought of Alex, of her generous nature. He remembered the feel of her hair on his chest . . .

He had wanted to bury his face in it. Her lips, he wanted
to taste them until they were swollen from his kisses.

He wanted to be with her, to be her husband.

And wasn't it pointless to have such notions? Eventually
he'd have to tell her about his past, then he could lose her
forever. He pushed the annoying thought out of his head.
Perhaps it was a good time to reveal his true self to her.
Maybe then she would stop looking at him with those wide
brown eyes. Asking him for something he could not give.

"That's quite a scowl," Cal said, his voice low.

"Why aren't you asleep?" Matt asked in exasperation,
opening his eyes, banishing Alex's image.

"I'm not used to sleeping in a bed so fine."

"We shouldn't be here," Matt said solemnly. "We should
go."

"Oh, no," Cal protested. "I didn't come four miles, freezing myself to death to turn around and leave. The Parkers
invited us to stay. It would be rude to decline."

Matt sat up. "I've never slept in a bed this soft in my
life." He felt as though he was in some sort of dream and
would wake up only to want more . . . and be denied.

"Enjoy it while it lasts. I'm going to get some sleep. I
suggest you do the same," Cal said, pulling the covers over
his head.

A log in the grate toppled, spitting orange sparks up the
chimney. The sun would be rising soon and he had to make
some decisions. He stared at the ceiling, hoping to find
some answers in the swirl of the plaster as Cal's soft snores
echoed through the still air. Matt grinned; so much for his
friend being unable to sleep.

Footsteps beyond the closed door alerted him. He
watched as the door handle turned slowly, and he closed
his eyes, pretending sleep as the scent of roses permeated

the air. The last thing he wanted at that moment was to face Alex. He knew he owed her more apologies—first for how he had behaved in the pilothouse, then for kissing her in front of the fire. Although he hadn't been quite lucid at the time, one thing he remembered for certain was that she kissed him back. Wholeheartedly. Now what did he make of that?

Soft footsteps passed his bed, heading toward the fireplace. He cracked open one eye and saw Alex put another log on the fire. She turned and he slammed his lid closed. Her scent became stronger as she approached the bed. He breathed in deeply, released, feigning sleep.

He almost jumped when she sat down next to him and placed, first, a hand on his forehead, and then ever so gently, her fingers through his hair. She smoothed the hair from his forehead, pushing it back. With one of her fingers, she traced his jaw line, and his heart nearly leaped clear out of his chest. What had he done to deserve her compassion?

She leaned toward him, over him. He could *sense* her there, hovering, even though she was no longer touching him. What was she doing? He fought hard to keep his body from betraying him, but when she ever so slowly used the pad of her thumb to caress his bottom lip, he flinched.

Keeping up the appearance of being asleep, he slapped at her hand as he would a gnat or fly, but he couldn't disguise the chill bumps along his arms and hoped she didn't notice them.

He felt her weight shift on the bed as she leaned even closer. "You scare me to death," she whispered.

He tensed. He couldn't help it. How had he frightened her? Insulted her, yes; he had done that quite well. But frighten?

"I'm so afraid of the way you make me feel. The way I

want to touch you. The way," she said so softly, "I want you to touch me. I don't know what to think about you coming here. Why, Matthew?" she whispered. "I had resigned myself to losing you forever."

The blood rushed through his head, blocking all other sounds as her sweet voice trailed off. He didn't hear Cal, or the fire, nor even his own deep, even breaths. He longed for her to keep speaking, to tell him more, to reveal herself to him in his "sleep."

Her hand caressed his face. His cheeks heated beneath her touch. Her voice startled him as she spoke again, softly, soothing. "I'm sorry for your pain, Matthew. I know how much you loved your boat. But in a sense I'm also glad for this tragedy, because it brought you back to me. And perhaps I am the person you need most right now, in more ways than one."

The bed tilted and he knew she had stood up. Quite gently she placed a kiss on his forehead and turned to leave the room. He waited until he heard the soft click of the door latching before he exhaled deeply.

And perhaps I am the person you need most right now, in more ways than one. What had she meant by that? Matt wondered as her parting words bounced through his thoughts.

"Holy Mother," Cal said under his breath.

Matt hadn't noticed that his snoring had stopped.

"If you don't marry that woman, you're the biggest fool I've ever met."

He hoped that if he kept quiet long enough Cal would think he was asleep.

"Don't think you're fooling me. I know you're awake; I can practically hear your pulse pounding from over here."

His pulse *was* pounding. His skin, tingling.

"She's too good for me," he breathed out.

"Her opinion, obviously, differs."

Matt heaved a pillow at him. "Shut up." Miraculously, he did, leaving Matt to his most private and terrifying thoughts.

If you don't marry that woman, you're the biggest fool I've ever met.

Alex's words also came back to him: *A marriage in name only, Matthew. I become your wife, and you get the Amazing Grace.*

He pulled the pillow over his head, wincing as his wound caught on the case. Marriage. It terrified him, yet he knew it was the only solution.

He would agree to Alex's inane proposal and marry her.

What would she say when he asked her to be his wife— for he knew he would be the one to do the asking this time around. His earlier refusal had hurt her deeply. More than if he had hit her, he had hurt her, knew it even before he heard Jonah's report of her heartbreaking sobs, crouched next to a riverfront warehouse after he'd sent his young crewman to follow her to be sure she returned safely home.

He pushed his face in his hands, hating himself. Couldn't she see that he was no good for her? Perhaps she did. She wanted marriage in name only. She wanted to be his wife on paper only. No bedroom privileges.

By marrying her he would be denying himself all he'd ever longed for. A family. But she needed him to save her family home, and he, he silently admitted, needed her. Her boat, to be exact, if he ever wanted to be on the river again.

Plus, he owed her. For her kindness, her compassion. Simply for the way she looked at him, as though she was clearly able to see the kind of man he wished himself to be.

Well, he thought, rolling over. That settled it. He would be the best fake husband there was to be had.

He groaned as he pulled the pillow over his head.

Chapter Ten

"This," Matthew announced, pausing and pointing to a wooden platform leading onto the cargo deck of the *Amazing Grace*, "is the stage."

Alex cleared her throat and said dryly, "Do we perform productions here also? Some Shakespeare, perhaps?"

Did he think them daft? Hearing the soft lapping of the river against the pilings, she absently wondered how her husband would like another swim in the icy Ohio.

His frown conveyed that he did not find her sense of sarcasm enjoyable. At least not today. Not, it seemed, since four days ago when they exchanged vows—shouted them, really, to the almost deaf reverend. The vows had been exchanged, but there had been no emotion put forth behind them from either of them. Just words, said aloud. Her heart ached.

When he had come to her and proposed—gruffly, but rather sweetly, in her opinion—she had thought marriage would change Matthew's surly behavior. She apparently thought wrong. Sorely wrong. She chastised herself. What had she expected? She knew full well he married her only for the boat. He had made that quite clear when he came to her the morning after his boat had exploded and proposed to her using the same terms she had brought to him the day before. A marriage in name only. He'd keep the boat; she'd buy back her house; they would go their separate ways.

A plan so tidy and simple, it needed only a bright red bow to complete the package, but she hadn't factored in one thing. She loved him. She knew it the moment he'd fallen at her feet the night his boat had exploded, the night she feared she'd lose him forever.

She sighed. Twenty-eight days. That was all she had to make the marriage work, to make him love her in return.

"She doesn't look as big as last time," Lou said from behind her, staring up at the *Amazing Grace*.

Jack's cowboy hat shadowed her eyes. "Because she's in the water."

The steamboat stood four stories high, its twin smokestacks jutting proudly into the cloudless sky. They were standing on the bottom deck, which she knew was called the Main Deck, dutifully following Matthew as he gave them a tour and introduced the crew.

She craned her neck, her eyes tracing the twin stacks of the *Amazing Grace*. She let her excitement build, overruling her concerns about her future, her marriage. She could understand her father's passion for the boat. So simple, it was majestic.

Matthew led them up several sets of steps to the Texas Deck, where the staterooms were located. He paused in the wide hallway and indicated which rooms were Jack's and

Lou's. Alex realized in sudden alarm that her quarters would now be shared with Matthew. The last four days she had spent in her own bed—alone—but now, now they would have to be together or risk questions from the crew that were unanswerable without sounding foolish.

She took it as a good sign when he took her hand as he neared a door at the end of a long hallway. Day one of twenty-eight and they were already handholding. It was a start, wasn't it?

"Normally, I sleep in the Captain's quarters with the crew, but it is not fit for two."

His hand was warm as it clasped hers. Calluses scratched her palm, eliciting delicious little sensations. She tried to ignore the feelings, ignore that he was simply being polite by offering his hand. She wanted to pretend he loved her, that she truly was his wife. What would she be feeling now as he opened their bedroom door if she were? Certainly not absolute, unadulterated fear, which was the emotion dampening her palms and tightening her throat as he pushed open the stateroom door.

"This will have to do," he said, gesturing to a large but sparsely furnished room.

Her gaze immediately sought the bed, then dropped to the floor as she realized how utterly large the mattress was. She couldn't bring herself to look at him, and cursed herself a fool as her cheeks enflamed.

"You can put them right here, Jonah," Matthew said to the crewman who had brought up her luggage. Matthew had informed her that Jonah had been a crew member on the *Muddy Waters,* and she had learned that her husband was very fond of the young man. She could see why. Standing side by side, the two had a very close resemblance. Perhaps Matthew saw himself in the younger man's eyes?

She would ask him one day. When he was more open to speaking to her about personal matters.

She looked around the room as Matthew sent Jonah on his way. Her few personal possessions took up little space. She tried not to think of leaving all she knew behind in River Glen, but the memories of leaving the house, her home, most of her possessions behind came rushing back. The bare walls, the echoing rooms.

Her chin lifted as she remembered that the house wasn't gone forever. She would buy it back. It would remain in the family. It had to.

"Alex, are you well?" Matthew asked.

She forced a smiled. "I am."

He picked up a small bag and placed it on the floor next to a threadbare sofa. "I'll be sleeping here, if you were worried."

"That's fine."

She had been worried, but didn't admit it. But now, as she looked between him, the bed, and the couch, she wondered why. He was, after all, her husband.

In name only, she reminded herself crossly.

Matthew lifted one of her satchels. "What do you have in here? Rocks?"

She smiled. "No. Journals. I write down stories I hear to pass on to—"

She had been about to say "my children" but stopped herself in time. "I like to write down stories I hear. Most of them were stories my father told."

He looked uncomfortable, and she had the uneasy feeling he recognized her slip-up. "I—that's good. Real good."

"I'd love to hear the stories your mother told you and write them down as well."

He stared at her for a long moment. Gruffly, he said, "Someday."

As he settled her luggage on the bed for unpacking, she twisted her wedding band, not used to the weight on her finger. Delicately etched with small rosebuds, the ring itself confused her all the more. Matthew had obviously taken a good deal of time to choose it, and if she was any judge of fine jewelry, had paid handsomely for it. Why? Why if their marriage was not to be real?

She didn't want to think of the possibilities, to have her hopes raised only to be dashed later. The ring, though, reminded her of an errand she had to run before they left port.

"When do we leave?" she asked.

"We back out in an hour. I need to go up to the pilot-house to review the course."

"May I sit with you up there? Maybe someday you can teach me to pilot her too."

His eyes widened. "You're joking."

"No."

Outside, a whistle blew. "You need a pilot's license, Alex. It is not something to be learned in a day."

She put her hands on her hips. "Then it's a good thing we have many days, isn't it?"

He mumbled something that sounded like "insufferable," and stormed past her and out the door.

She winced as the door closed, even though it hadn't slammed. She would learn to pilot the *Amazing Grace.* She'd hound Matthew until he taught her. She smiled thinking of it. He was bound to put up a fight. It seemed as though a big ball of frustration at her false marriage had taken root in her ribcage. She was dying to let it loose. And

Captain Kinkade, with his cranky disposition, was just the man to take the brunt of her anger.

Where was she? Matt wondered as he paced the length of the stage. The wood vibrated beneath his feet. The boilers were fired up, the passengers, what few they had, were loaded, the hogs, smell and all, were safely secured in the cargo hold of the Main Deck. They were ready to leave. Except Miss Alexandra Park—Mrs. Alex Kinkade was nowhere to be found.

Not that he blamed her. He'd been surly and rude to her these past few days, even after he vowed to himself to be a kind and patient husband.

Not that it was his fault. A man could take only so much. Why had she gone and looked at him calf's eyes during their wedding ceremony? She looked as though she was looking forward to being his wife. But if that was true, why had she made it clear that their marriage would be in name only?

He reminded himself that in name only was the way he preferred their union. To become man and wife in every sense of the word would mean having to tell her of his past, which was the last thing he wanted to do. For if he did, he'd surely lose her forever. He needed to keep his distance, he told himself. Telling himself, however, did no good. Whenever he was close to her, he felt the need to touch her.

He shook his head. What a convoluted situation this turned out to be. She who looked at him with stars in her eyes, but demanded a platonic relationship, and he who would gladly touch her if her permission was granted but for his past . . . What a pair they were.

He let out a loud sigh.

Pacing the decking, he kept an eye out for her as he recalled their first night as man and wife. He had gone to his room, and she to hers, without even a goodnight kiss to send him off to sleep. It was more than he could bear. His mood only darkened from that point on, till now when it felt as though his nerves were going to snap from the stress of keeping his hands to himself and off his own wife.

"That's quite a frown, Captain."

He spun and released a deep breath of relief. Too lost in his thoughts, he hadn't seen nor heard her approach.

"Where have you been?" he demanded, leading her onto the boat. Immediately the crew raised the stage after them.

She said nothing as she loosened the ties of her bonnet.

The simple gesture stole his breath. Memories of their kiss in the pilothouse were quick to come into focus. His emotions jumbled, causing him to feel as though he were lost in a huge maze and there was only one exit: Alex, herself. And that wasn't an option for him. He just had to keep looking for another way out.

Forcing himself to brush away his feelings for her, he said, "We had to delay our departure."

"It couldn't be helped," she returned without apology.

Her dark gaze challenged him to continue hounding her. He wanted to. Wanted to fight with her, have it all out in the open. His feelings, her feelings. Their different backgrounds. And most importantly, why they should never have married, especially under the pretenses of in name only. He had the sinking sensation, though, that she would counterattack his every point with one of her own. Neither would win because he was quickly learning that when it came to stubbornness, he had met his match.

"Come with me to the pilothouse."

She followed his command without comment, which surprised him. She seemed to have a will of her own and knew how to use it against him. Truly, she rarely did as he bid.

"We have a schedule to keep," he reminded. "Cal's in a tizzy as it is. He arranged to pick up some lumber from a mill in Louisville."

"How wonderful."

"It is, if we can make it in time." His accusing tone hung in the air, a silent gauntlet.

Calmly, she replied, "As I said, it couldn't be helped."

"That's all the explanation I get?"

She smiled sweetly. "That's all the explanation you deserve."

He opened his mouth to argue with her but closed it again, knowing it was futile. As the whistles blew their departure, he stepped into the pilothouse, and took control of the wheel from young Jonah who had been keeping watch.

Using a set of tubes, he called down to the boiler room. Within moments the boat shuddered, shaking to life as it backed away from Cincinnati, inky smoke pouring from its stacks.

Alex's face shone with excitement as she peered out the windows. His chest grew warm. She was his. His! Until death. At the time he had simply said the words, but hadn't truly meant them. However, the longer he was with her, the more he began to believe them true.

He set a straight course down the river, heading toward Louisville. There were several coal flats on the water, but no other steamers. This boat wasn't the *Muddy Waters*, but it would do. The investigation into the *Muddy Waters'* accident had found no known cause for the explosion, which in itself was highly suspicious to Matt's way of thinking; there was always a reason somewhere among the debris and witnesses. The explosion was ruled accidental, which meant that he would receive the insurance money, but it also meant that however Simson—and Matt felt certain Simson was somehow connected—had sabotaged the *Muddy Waters* would never be learned, nor would Simson ever be publicly accused.

Removing his coat and hat as the wood stove warmed the pilothouse, he swept a hand through his hair. The white bandage still covered his healing wound and he grimaced when he realized the cut would soon need to be cleaned. Although Lou had a gentle touch, the ointment she used stung.

Alex's back was to him as she looked out at the river, but he could see the outline of her profile. The cold had teased color into her cheeks, her lips. Curls lay pinned to the back of her head, but more than a few strands had escaped their confines and twisted down her back. Why she continually tried to keep her hair up was beyond his reasoning. Why not just wear it down if that was where it longed to be?

Scanning her attire, he felt his stomach tighten. He knew that she could not know that blue was his favorite color, but he liked to think she had chosen the blouse for him.

He couldn't seem to help looking at her, drinking her in. The way she looked, the way she smelled of lemons and roses, the way her breath caught on every third or fourth inhalation. The window just beyond her mouth would fog, then clear, with every other breath. Fog, clear. It was almost as though he could feel her hot breath on his neck.

He tugged at his collar as the pilothouse seemed to close in around him. Fog, clear. He watched her mouth, mesmerized. Realizing he was staring at her lips and wishing that they were on his, he expelled a deep sigh and made himself look away.

Again, he pushed his hand through the hair he had left as he turned his attention back to the dark ripples of the river.

Jack and Lou, as far as he knew, were safely ensconced on the Texas Deck, away from the other crew, who had taken an immediate liking to the Parker sisters. Shaking his head, he knew this trip was going to test his patience. It already had with Alex's disappearance.

Moving at a good clip, the *Amazing Grace* pushed through the water, its side paddles propelling it forward through the murky Ohio River. It wouldn't be long before they were in Louisville. After loading the extra cargo, they would continue south during the night.

Glancing up, he saw Alex looking at him. For a beat, his heart lay still in his chest. There was such utter longing on her face that a man would have to be blind not to see it.

But what did the longing in her eyes mean? He was so confused at her conflicting actions. Her eyes told him one thing, her voice another. A marriage in name only, she had said. He pretended to ignore the look. He didn't want to jump to the conclusion that she wanted more to their marriage than she originally offered.

"You asked me where I was," she said, her voice smooth, even.

"And you told me that I didn't deserve an answer, insufferable woman that you are," he returned with a wry grin.

Her lips curved into a smile that stole his breath. "I needed to make a purchase."

"I thought we were all set. Food, linen—"

"Not for the *Amazing Grace*."

His palms dampened. "Then what?"

"For you."

He looked at her for the briefest moment, then turned away. Sharply, he reminded himself that he could never become her husband in the true sense, even if she wished it. There was a purity to her he never wanted to tarnish. And knowing about his past would surely darken her spirit. He would be her friend. He could do that, be that. Her friendship was more than he'd ever expected in the first place.

"Really?" he said, trying to seem uninterested and not doing a very good job of it.

She rose and stood next to him, her elbow bumping his. "I was remiss a few days ago. I admit I hadn't thought too far ahead when I approached you with my proposal."

She held out her hand. A wide orb of gold lay in her palm. A ring. A wedding band. He swallowed over the sudden tightness in his throat.

"I'm sorry," she apologized, "that it isn't as fancy as mine. I—There was not enough money . . ." Her voice trailed off as she looked at him. "I hope it fits."

Such willpower it took not to take her in his arms, to devour her in hot kisses, to taste her silky skin. He longed to know what it would be like to wake up every morning next to her, to lay next to her every night as they fell asleep, to see her heavy with his child, to witness the changes of her body. He wanted it all, and knew he could have no more than friendship from her if he was to protect her from his past.

Since he made no move to take the ring from her, she hesitantly lifted his left hand and slid the ring on his fourth finger. It fit perfectly. She gave his fingers a squeeze as she released her grip.

"Thank you," he managed to say. For some reason, speaking had become very difficult.

"You're welcome."

She remained next to him, her elbow still touching his. He knew he had to put distance between them. Being this close to her, seeing that loving, dare he say, *wifely*, look in her eye, hurt him, for he wanted her so badly and knew that she would truly never be his.

He could deal with the lingering pain that was his childhood—he had learned over time how to dull that ache, but this pain . . . He was defenseless against it; it wounded him to his very soul.

He had good reason to push her away, he knew, but as Alex kept looking at him with those warm brown eyes of hers, he couldn't help himself. He reached for her with his one free arm, the other keeping the pilot wheel on course, and pulled her close. Gently he covered her lips with his own, tasting but for a brief moment, but enough, just barely enough, to ease the growing hunger inside him. "Thank you," he whispered, "for the ring. It's a perfect fit."

Breathlessly, she said, "You're still welcome."

The wheel tugged at him, and he shifted his focus from her to the river, all the while calling himself every kind of fool for breaking his promise to himself to keep her at arm's length.

She remained by his side, watching him with those expectant eyes of hers. Swallowing twice, he cleared his throat. He knew the words he was about to speak were not the ones he wanted to tell her. He longed to speak words of love, or at least hope. And after that brief but intense kiss, they were words she deserved. Words he wanted to gift her with. But wouldn't. Couldn't.

"Quite a day. I think our schedule isn't off by much. If

we catch a nice wind, we might be able to make it to Louisville ahead of schedule."

She lowered her lids and turned her gaze back to the
window, to the scenery passing by, to the bleakness of the
winter landscape.

He swallowed again, his heart beating strongly against
his ribs. It was shouting for him to say it. To tell her he
cared for her, that he might even love her. "Alex?"

"Yes?" Curiosity lit the corners of her eyes as she turned
toward him.

"I . . ."

Patiently she waited while he fought an inner battle.
Somehow he had fallen in love with his wife. He remembered the way she cared for him, her gentle touch. He admired her fierce determination to do what was best for her
sisters. Just from the weeks he'd known her he saw that
she never did anything half-heartedly. She gave life everything she had, and had yet to get anything in return.

He kept his gaze on the water, always seeking a snag or
other disaster looming. His life had been lived much the
same way. Always looking for the next tragedy to befall
him. His father had died at war. His mother died of fever
when he was seven. He'd lived his childhood on the streets,
until that fateful night . . .

Shaking his head, he refused to think of it. It wasn't until
his escape to the river that he felt somewhat at peace. He
was a loner by nature, a man hardened by his life. And it
wasn't until he'd met Alex Parker that he felt he could
allow love into his life.

He had never believed it possible to fall for someone so
quickly. The nights were long aboard a steamer and he'd
often heard stories of sudden love from the sailors, a love

that hit so hard it stole one man's breath, and had knocked another to his knees, but Matt had never believed it.

Until now.

Sneaking at glance at Alex, he wondered if he deserved such a woman. Deserving or not she was his wife now, he reminded himself. Didn't she have a right to know of his past? No longer did he want to hide it. He wanted to tell her, to tell her all about himself. He'd never wanted to share himself with another before, but perhaps if he told Alex, they might have a future . . . if he didn't scare her away.

If he didn't lose her.

"There's more to me than you think," he blurted.

Surprise filled him as she smiled, a small laugh escaping her lips. "I should hope so, Captain."

His eyebrows dipped. "You don't understand."

"Then tell me so I do understand, and we can get past it, Matthew."

"When I was young," he began.

The sound of someone on the stairs silenced him. Cal McQue came bustling into the pilothouse.

He looked between the two of them, must have sensed the tension. "Did I interrupt?"

Alex rose and moved toward the door. "Not at all." She turned her gaze to Matt. "It shall wait. I'll be seeing you at supper, Captain?"

She gazed at him, long and hard, making him uncomfortable with her scrutiny. Biting her lips, she looked as though she wanted to tell him something, but she simply waited for his reply. "Yes," he said, his voice cracking on the single word.

She smiled and went out the door.

"What was that about?" Cal asked.

"That was me about to make the biggest mistake of my life."

Chapter Eleven

Alex made enough noise as she went down the steps to be heard, she was sure, three decks down. Quietly, she tiptoed back up them and crept toward the door, bent low to keep out of sight. She pressed her ear close to the door she had purposely left ajar and listened to the conversation inside the pilothouse.

Her conscience nagged that eavesdropping was wrong, but she was determined to get some answers about her husband and hoped this little bit of trickery would prove fruitful.

She heard Matthew say, "That was me about to make the biggest mistake of my life."

"How so?" Cal said.

There was silence for a moment. Then her husband spoke. "I was about to tell her of my past."

"I think that's wise."

"I thought so too for a moment, but no longer."

Alex drew her coat closer around her neck, fighting off the chill wind.

"If I tell her," Matthew said, "I will lose her. And Cal, I don't want to lose her. I can't jeopardize my marriage."

She heard footsteps within and shrank against the wood paneling of the boat.

"But what kind of marriage can you have if you don't tell her?"

What was it that he was keeping from her? She couldn't imagine him, a man who looked at her with his heart in his eyes, could have done anything that would make her not want to be with him.

Matthew's voice rose. "If I tell her I will lose her, and then I'll have no marriage at all."

"She's a special woman, Matt."

"I know."

"I think it's safe to say she loves you."

Alarm slipped through Alex's veins. Had she been so obvious?

Cal continued. "I see the way she looks at you, Matt. My mother used to look at my father that way. And the way she cared for you after the explosion . . ."

"She's not said a word to me."

"Perhaps she's afraid she'll be rejected."

Alex nodded beyond the door.

Matthew's voice sounded tortured. "And she would be."

Her hopes crumpled.

"Are you telling me you don't love her?" Cal demanded.

Her heart pounding in her ears, she kept still, not even daring to breathe for fear she'd miss his answer.

"No. I admit I love her. I don't know how it happened, but her spirit has captured my black heart."

Clamping a hand over her mouth, Alex fought not to cry out with joy.

"However, I can never tell her of my love. Because if I do, I'll have to tell her of my past. I'd rather her friendship than risk her being lost to me forever."

Alex slipped quietly down the steps, having heard enough. She paused at the landing, a smile playing on her lips.

A sense of calm washed through her, cleansing her of her earlier anxiety. She had hope, hope that all was not lost. The *Amazing Grace* would make it to New Orleans on time without any problems, and she and her sisters would be just fine. She and Matthew could make it work.

How quickly despair could change to giddiness.

He loved her.

More than once she had thought she'd seen it in his eyes, but wouldn't allow herself to hope.

He loved her. But feared losing her.

She strode down the hallway as she tried to guess what would be so bad in his past that he felt the need to shield her. As she walked along the deck, she admitted that he was a hard man. It was obvious in his stance, his eyes, that he had seen—and probably done—much he longed to forget. If it took all her patience, she would get him to open up to her, to tell her of his inner demons. He had to know that she wouldn't fault him for them, wouldn't he? How could she? The dealings of his past probably helped shape him into the fine man he was today.

Her husband.

Alex wondered if she should tell him of her feelings. Her pride had been so wounded by his earlier rejections that she wasn't eager to show him her hand just yet. And after hearing what he had just said she wasn't entirely sure he'd welcome her admission of love, being that he was convinced he couldn't have her.

So, she was going to fight for him. Fight with all her heart. Convince him that she did not need his protection, that she loved the man he had become. And oh, she would most certainly point out that he cared for her too. He had her fooled for a while with his facade of indifference, but now she knew how he really felt. And now, there was no stopping her.

With the feelings they had for each other, there was no reason they shouldn't have a true, real marriage. Worry tickled her stomach. Was her conviction enough to break through his resolve?

She made her way down from the pilothouse to the aft end of the Texas Deck and to their stateroom at the stern.

Inside the room, she laughed aloud, spinning in a circle. Happiness had been long absent in her life since her mother's death, and then her father's.

Abruptly, a fresh wave of guilt crushed her newfound happiness, stomped it into the ground. Swaying, she sat on the bed, sinking into the soft tick.

Her father had been dead less than a month and here she was wearing vibrant colors, spinning in laughter! What kind of person was she to be so shallow and heartless? Putting her head in her hands, she asked herself over and over the same question.

Flopping backward, she stared blankly at the ceiling, at the solid beams of wood crossing the room. Had she no right to be happy?

She thought of her father. Hiram Parker had been by no means a conventional man. Rather, unique. Giving, demanding. Loving, stern. His whole personality had seemed at odds with itself, yet for Hiram it had worked.

The steamboat swayed gracefully as it pushed full steam ahead toward Louisville. The *Amazing Grace*. Her father's boat. She hoped he was looking down on them, proud of his girls for making his dream come true. Sitting up, Alex realized her guilt was ebbing. She knew for certain her father wouldn't begrudge her happiness. Not in a million years. He loved her. Loved all of them, and wanted all of them to be happy. Hadn't he always told them never to settle on a man? To search until the right one was found?

With a smile curving her lips, she remembered his words from a day not too long ago, and wondered if somehow he knew she would need the words of wisdom. *Love is a battle. You need to fight hard, Alex, or it may be lost forever.* He had been so wise, her father, and she had been lucky to have him in her life.

Standing, she crossed to the window, stared at the clouds rolling in. She would fight for Matthew Kinkade. Weaken his defenses and let her love heal his heart. For somehow she knew it had been wounded before and this was one of the reasons he pushed her away.

It would be the battle of her lifetime, she was sure. She smiled. She was definitely up for the challenge.

Jack sat up, drew her knees to her chin. She gathered the thick blanket between her knees and leaned forward. "When I first heard of this boat, I was more than a little surprised that Father didn't tell us about it. Of course, I would have thought him crazy for wanting to be a pilot, but now that I'm here, on the *Amazing Grace*, I can understand why he enjoyed it so." She tucked a thick lock of black hair behind her ear. "There's a calm on the water. The way the wind tilts the boat, the noise of the paddlewheels, the water sloshing. Even the bell is comforting. It feels as though Father is here with us."

Lou nodded. "It does. I feel the same way."

Alex sat in a chair next to Jack's bed. By sitting with her sisters well into the night, she was delaying the inevitable. Her earlier vows to fight for Matthew had slowly weakened in a fit of nerves. How would he react when she came to him, and told him she wished to be wife in truth, not just for show? She couldn't quite picture him joyous, but rather easily the image of him banishing her from his life forever formed in her thoughts. She sighed silently.

"I think it's time we turned in," Lou said on a yawn.

They had arrived in Louisville on schedule, loaded the lumber, bought a few supplies, and were heading south now, toward the Mississippi River, which would bring them to New Orleans.

Supper had been an informal affair, since it happened to coincide with arriving in Louisville. Alex hadn't seen Matthew since earlier in the pilothouse. She'd had all day to let her thoughts manifest, her anxiety grow, her stomach turn into a giant jumble of knots.

What if he turned her away?

"Aren't you tired, Alex?" Jack asked as she brushed her hair.

"Nervous," she admitted on a whisper.

Jack's expression softened. "It will be okay. He said he would sleep on the sofa."

How did she tell her sisters that her nerves weren't based on Matthew staying away, but on doubts that he would never come near? She couldn't, so she kept her mouth closed, but she wasn't ready to leave—and to face her husband—quite yet.

"You seem to be spending much time with Mr. McQue," she said to Jack.

"He intrigues me, Alex."

"Why?"

Lou rolled over. "He's a gambler who refuses to admit it." She nibbled her lip and plucked at the pillow. "Apparently he is strictly high-stakes and loses more than he wins."

"Why does he keep denying his gambling ways?" Jack asked, as if Alex hadn't heard Lou say the same thing not seconds before.

She smiled. Jack must be totally smitten with the man. "He must be wondering how you know of him in the first place, since women aren't allowed in the gaming halls."

"True. I intend to find out why he's hiding the truth, though."

"Maybe he's just embarrassed." Alex rose, thinking it time she faced her own embarrassment.

"Perhaps."

She bid good-night to her sisters and stepped out into the hallway. The route she took to her own room was circuitous, leading her out to the open decking. Rain spit from the sky, and she tugged at her collar and wrapped her arms around herself.

Below her, Jonah walked the length of the Hurricane Deck, back and forth, on night watch duty. She called out a good-night, and he answered in kind.

Her stomach churned as she turned the handle on the stateroom door and she pushed it open. Warmth hit her in the face as she took a quick look around, confirming what her instincts had already told her: Matthew wasn't there. She sighed in relief as if she'd been given a reprieve.

She quickly changed into her nightclothes, wondering

where he could be. Was he avoiding her as she had done by staying so long with her sisters?

As she lay down in bed, pulling the covers up, she couldn't help but feel cowardly. What had happened to her grand plans of making Matthew admit his love?

Alex sat up. Despite his sudden kiss in the pilothouse this morning, it was perfectly obvious from Matthew's demeanor that he wouldn't be the one to come to her. She needed to make the first move. Maybe not tonight, nor tomorrow, but soon. As soon as the knot in her stomach unraveled.

Blowing out a deep breath, she realized she didn't want to go sleep without at least bidding Matthew good-night. She slipped on her robe and slippers and exited the room in search of her wayward spouse.

She found him in the pilothouse.

The knot in her stomach made her hands shake, so she headed straight to the wood stove where she warmed her fingers. "Good evening, Matthew."

He stole a look at her over his shoulder, his gaze roaming from her hair, which fell in waves across her back, to the tips of her slipper-covered toes. His gray eyes narrowed, a heat in them that warmed her quicker than the fire. His gaze bolstered her courage as she felt a few of her stomach knots disappearing.

Finally he said, "Evenin'. A bit late for you to be up and about, isn't it?" He turned back to the river.

"I could say the same to you," she said as she stepped up next to him.

He winked at her. "Truly insufferable, you are," he said with a smile.

She rolled her eyes. "I came to say good-night." As she turned toward the river, she gasped when she realized there was no window in front of the pilot wheel. The rain seemed to blow in on every gust of wind, splashing everything in sight, including her and Matthew.

"What happened to the window?"

"Removable. Can't see a thing if the pane's dripping with water."

"Aren't you cold?"

"No."

"Do you need a coat?" she asked, eyeing his broad shoulders and the thick shirt covering them. Raindrops splattered across the fabric on his chest.

"No," he said curtly.

She bit her lip. Sometimes, she decided, she wished to smack the back of his head just for the fun of it. His one-word answers were infuriating, but now Alex knew better than to be put off by his gruff exterior.

He loved her.

She wanted to confront him with the knowledge but bit her lip. She wasn't ready. What if he denied it? When the time was right, she would make him tell her the truth.

Taking a seat on the lazy bench, as she now knew it was called, she wiped the moisture from her face using her fingers. The wooden bench stretched the length of the pilothouse, about ten feet, and was where everyone except the pilot sat.

"Are you worried about the storm?" she asked, desperate for something to say, and not wanting to leave just yet.

"No."

If it wasn't for the white bandage on his head, she thought she would have hit him. If he had simply made pleasant conversation, she might have left him alone. But his one-word answers blended inside of her a sudden burst of annoyance and a hint of anger, creating a boldness she never knew existed.

Slowly she rose and stepped up behind him, close but not touching. So close, in fact, that she could feel the heat of his body radiating through his shirt, and the tensing of his muscles as he felt her presence.

Carefully nestling her head between his shoulder blades, she wrapped her arms around him, her hands splaying across his chest. She heard the clink of metal as her wedding band nipped one of his buttons.

Feeling his back stiffen in surprise, she smiled, knowing he couldn't see it. She heard his deep intake of breath and pressed a little bit tighter. The warmth of his body felt comforting, right.

"Do you have a penchant for sleepwalking?" he asked in a halting voice.

"No."

"Are you trying to make me hit a sandbar and sink the boat?"

Ah, she thought, full sentences at last. "Why would I want to do that? I can't swim."

He took hold of her arm and pulled her to the side so he could see her face.

She was disappointed in his abrupt manner, but kept it out of her eyes. The decision had been made to be forward with him, and she wasn't about to turn back now. He loved her, of that Alex was certain. She just didn't know how to make him tell her so.

"You can't swim?"

"No."

"You have to learn," he ordered.

"I don't want to," she said, stubbornly.

"Why not?"

She had her reasons, none of which she wanted to share with him. "Because I don't wish to, Matthew."

Leaving one hand on the pilot wheel, he pushed the other through his dark hair. The graying over his ears shimmered in the dim light of the pilothouse. Alex yearned to reach out and mimic his movements, but kept her hands at her sides. She'd made quite a fool of herself already.

"Alex, knowing how to swim is a matter of life and death on the river. You need to know how."

Stubbornly, she said, "No I don't."

"Are you afraid of the water?" he asked in a gentle tone she rarely heard. He'd used the same tone the morning he'd come to the house, the morning she had burned her hand.

"No." She stood straight, her back stiff. She was not going to learn to swim. There was no way she was going to dress in swimming attire and let the whole world see her gangly legs and overextended torso. Never. She'd rather die drowning.

She frowned at her logic. Here she was, trying to convince her husband that theirs should be a real marriage, yet she was terrified to let him see her body. Well, she deemed, if it ever came to that, she would simply turn out the lights. Under the comfort of darkness, she could do anything, and hide anything, she wished.

"This won't do, Alex. You need to learn to swim. What if we sink?"

"I have perfect confidence that you'll save me."

He moaned and swiped his hand through his hair again. She noticed that he had the habit of doing so when he was frustrated. Which, it seemed, was often when he was in her presence. A small grin curved her lips. It was another clue she had missed regarding his feelings for her.

"Why are you smiling?"

"Because you're frustrated," she answered honestly.

"And that makes you happy?"

"Sometimes, Matthew," she said softly. She drew in a deep breath. "When I know . . . I know it means you *do* care for me. More than you let on."

A muscle ticked in his jaw. "Nonsense," he barked, and focused his gaze on the river.

Alex also noticed his tendency to get louder when she touched a little too close to the truth. Walking over to the fire, she stood close, letting the flames warm her.

His voice came out low, but hard-edged. "I think it best if you go to bed, Alex. Anyone could walk in and make assumptions."

"What kind of assumptions?" she baited. "We're married." She really shouldn't be enjoying this conversation, but she was. How had she not seen it before? Each of his quirks, the loudness, the crankiness . . . it was all an act. An act designed to keep her from knowing he cared about her. She wanted to laugh aloud, hug him, and kiss him all at once.

As she watched his stiff posture though, tenderness swept through her. He cared for her. Really cared. *What* had happened in his past that made him so afraid to love?

He mumbled under his breath. She didn't hear the words, but could imagine he probably called her insufferable, for it was fast becoming his favorite description of her, and she was slowly coming to recognize it as his way of being—dare she think it?—playful.

She crossed her arms over her chest to keep from reaching out and touching his hair that fell on the back of his shirt collar most enticingly. The ends of the dark locks curled slightly, resting just above his shoulders. It was longer than it had been the last time she was alone in the pilothouse with him.

Closing her eyes, she remembered the feel of his locks in her hands, his lips on hers, the feel of his fingers as they caressed her face.

Her eyes opened and she found him watching her. A log shifted in the stove, creating sparks. Appropriate, Alex thought, feeling as though if a match were lit the room would explode from the tension stretching between them.

Ever so softly, he said, "What are you thinking about with that look on your face, Alex?"

She should just bite her tongue and let the question pass, but she had never been one to do what she should. Wanting him to know, wanting to see his reaction, she walked over next to him to get a better view of his face, and said, "I was thinking about the first time we were in the pilothouse alone, Matthew. I was thinking about the way we kissed."

She was rewarded with a darkening of his eyes, and yet another swipe of his hand through his hair. Their gazes locked.

He didn't shift his gaze, but he said, "I'm afraid that was a mistake." He swallowed. "I . . . You were so beautiful, with that hair and those eyes . . . I couldn't resist."

Sudden tears sprang to Alex's eyes. He'd called her beautiful. Though her chest ached with the need to simply hold him, she knew she was too close to him admitting the truth to dwell on his sweet words.

With great reluctance, she resumed her position on the lazy bench. "*Was* it a mistake, Matthew? What about the second time we kissed? The third?"

The muscle in his jaw continued to tick. His knuckles turned white as he gripped the pilot wheel as though it were about to roll away. "Look," he said with enough false cheer that she smiled. "Rain's stopping."

"A change of subject won't help you now, Matthew." Slowly, she repeated, "Was it a mistake to kiss me, to kiss your wife?" She rose from the bench, and positioned herself next to him. Gently, she touched his chin, stilling the muscle tick, lightly running her finger over his dimple. "You wouldn't let me kiss you again? A good-night kiss?"

He shifted on his feet, clearly uncomfortable. "You're playing with fire, honey."

"It's a good thing I happen to like the heat."

He took a quick look at the river, then reached out to her, drawing her close. "Lord knows I've tried to resist, but I can't."

He kissed her forehead, her cheeks, the column of her throat. Blood rushed through her ears, causing her to sway. He pulled her even more tightly as he rained gentle kisses on her upturned face.

"Why, Matthew, why resist me?"

She stared into his eyes, and nearly melted with the heat dancing in them. He lowered his lips, nipping at hers.

"At this moment," he grumbled, "I can't remember. Ask . . . me . . . later." His lips lowered to hers.

Her legs went weak, her heart doubled its beats, and the most wonderful warmth seeped into her body. She wrapped her hands around his neck and kissed him back, showing with the gentle action what she was still too afraid to say aloud.

He pulled back, a tortured look in his eyes. "Alex, I—"

Pounding footsteps preceded the door of the pilothouse being flung open. Matthew tucked her slightly behind him, protectively.

Jonah stood panting in the doorway. He tipped his head

to her before fixing his gaze on a spot above Matthew's head, and said, "Ma'am."

Matthew's words came out in a jagged rush. "Jonah, what's wrong?"

"They need you below, Captain."

"What's happened?" Matthew demanded.

"The hogs . . . they're dyin'."

Chapter Twelve

Matt clenched his teeth. Usually when he was mad, he raged, bellowing and shouting. Not now. Silent anger burned through his veins. Forty hogs had died. Forty!

He pushed both hands into his hair, the fingers of his left hand gliding carefully over his almost healed wound. When Lou had removed the sutures early that morning he had sensed a shift in her personality. Normally reserved, that morning she had been talkative, inquisitive.

By Lou's actions, he knew that Alex had not told her sisters of the hogs. By her tone, he knew she was trying very subtly, and not very well, he might add, to pry into his past. What had his family been like? Where had he gone to school? When had he decided on a life on the river? Did he like opera? Was he originally from Ohio?

Too many questions. Thankfully over the years he had become quite good at avoidance. His answers had been vaguely honest. Telling his sister-in-law the truth was out of the question: His father had died before he was born, his mother when he was seven; he never went to school, but learned to read from Aiden, the man who tended the bar above the basement room in which he spent most of his nights; that he used to go to the river for comfort and it was an easy escape after almost being caught breaking into a bakery. Opera? He used to beg for money from the people going into Cincinnati's large opera house, but he never, ever went inside. How would he tell her that he had grown up miles from her, yet a world apart?

Like a pesky bee, Lou had kept at it and wondered if Alex had sent her, seeking information. He wouldn't put it past his unconventional wife.

He had to admit Lou's tactics were good. She had a way about her that elicited information. But he was better. He knew more ways to avoid a direct question than she knew how to press. Eventually she gave up, knowing little more than she had when she came in.

A ray of sunshine beamed through his window, illuminating a patch of rug. The rug was, he speculated, originally a rich maroon. Now, it was a dull pinkish color. The whole interior of the steamboat needed an overhaul. But first they would need to decide what to do with the *Amazing Grace*. Use her solely as a packet—a passenger and freight boat? Freight only? Passenger only? It was a decision that would have to be put off until the goods they currently carried were delivered.

He bent over his desk, turning his attention to the boat's ledgers. He needed to determine how badly the loss of forty heads of hogs would affect their finances. A knock sounded. He looked up with anticipation, then cursed his heart and the way its beating increased. He was grateful the betrayal of his feelings was internal and easily hid from Alex's prying eyes.

"Enter."

The door pushed open and surprisingly, Cal—not his wife—came in and strode straight to the liquor cabinet. He poured himself a large tumbler full of whiskey, drank it, and laughed, long and hard. "You're in for it, Matt. After spending this past week with that family of yours, I've come to understand one thing. Those Parker girls like to get their way."

"What do you mean?" He knew exactly what he meant, but was curious about Cal's take on Jack, Lou, and Alex.

"Take Jack Parker for example. Twice now she has forced her way into the crew's card game. Cleaned them out, too," he said with awe.

"She shouldn't be allowed in the crew's quarters." Matt thought of all the things that could happen to a pretty young girl alone with twenty crewmen. Not that he thought his crew would take advantage of her, but they were, after all, human.

"She seems quite able to care for herself." He frowned. "She also seems to be convinced I'm a gambling man."

Matt chuckled. "Well, you are."

"I know, but no one's supposed to know that. I go to gaming clubs in disguise. Hats, fancy clothes, a mustache, for heaven's sake. And how does she know? She couldn't have possibly been there."

Suddenly a snippet of conversation played in Matt's mind. Words to the effect of Jack dressing as a man to gamble . . . It seemed too impossible to be true, but he had come to expect the unexpected where the three sisters were concerned.

"I don't know."

"I don't like it, Captain. If she starts asking questions, I could be in real danger."

"Then tell her the truth."

"That would put her in danger. I couldn't do that to her."

Matt laughed again. "Hmmm. Sounds suspiciously like mooning."

Cal colored but said nothing. Matt felt pity for his friend. Falling for a Parker was like stepping into the path of a tornado.

Cal shook his head. "You're dreaming." He quickly changed the subject. "And Lou . . ."

"What about her?" Lou seemed so sweet and innocent to Matt, which surely proved she had to have a hidden side. She was, after all, a Parker.

"The dumbwaiter? Well, she had the bright idea that it would be fun to ride up to the Texas Deck from the galley."

The pen fell from his fingers. "She didn't."

"Oh, she did. Sweet-talked the galley hands into letting her do it, too." Cal raked his fingers over his face in frustration. "She's a nice girl, but she knows how to manipulate the men with that pretty smile of hers. And—"

Matt held up a hand to stall Cal's next report. "Don't tell me any more. I don't want to know." He was going to have to sit down with Jack and Lou, then he was going to have to issue orders that the crew not participate in the whimsies of his new sisters. Lord help him.

Cal sat down. He crossed his leg over his knee, keeping hold of his ankle. "I didn't want to ask, but the hogs . . . ?"

"Forty dead."

Cal winced. "A loss, but it could have been worse. Told Alex yet?"

"No."

A soft tap sounded at the door, and Alex called out a hesitant, "Matthew, are you in there?"

Standing, Cal said, "I really don't want to be around for this conversation."

"Neither do I," Matt mumbled as the door opened a crack, then all the way. Alex stepped into the room, and he inhaled deeply the scent of lemons and roses, released the air slowly.

Cal bid his good-days and slipped out the door without a backward glance.

Glancing up, he met her gaze. "About the hogs," he began.

She sat down in a rickety old chair that wobbled. "I heard they ate tainted food."

"Yes. We lost forty, but we still have plenty to fulfill our contract," he reassured her.

"Do we know how the food came to be tainted?"

He shook his head, telling himself to avoid her eyes. The deep brown always seemed to manage to reach down inside of him, past all the barriers.

"We'll probably never know. Their troughs have been cleaned, and I've men keeping a close eye on what's fed to them. They'll be fine. Everything will be fine," he said with more confidence than he felt.

He kept his gaze on his desk top, above her head, on the ledger—anywhere but her face. He heard the rustling of her clothes and knew she had shifted in her seat, but didn't dare look.

He picked up a pen. "We're still on schedule."

"You're sure?"

Was that doubt in her voice? Longing to look up, he looked down instead at his shoes. "Absolutely."

Silence lingered. She was staring at him; he could tell

by the way his chest tightened. He should mention something about what happened the night before . . . Really, he ought to, he thought, trying to bolster his courage. Unfortunately, he could find no words to describe how her kiss affected him so.

He kept his gaze trained on the ledger, so he wouldn't have to look at her. Too easily his resolve to keep his distance was lost when he looked at her. Especially today when she looked particularly lovely. Wearing a green high-collared shirt with black braiding down the front which fit her snugly at the waist, she stole his breath. As much as she looked stunning in blue, green was more her color.

Looking wholesome, natural, and stunningly beautiful, she was devastating his ability to keep his distance. She had a hold on him. A tight one. He just didn't know what to do about it.

He flipped a page in the ledger, columns of numbers blurring under his desperate stare.

"Could Simson be behind our misfortune?" she asked.

He did glance up then, because of the note of anger in her voice. Only when he looked up, she looked down. Her hair was parted in the middle, a thin white line amidst a riot of brown curls that were pulled back into some sort of knot at her neck.

He had known that looking at her would be his downfall. It felt as though Cupid's own arrow had shot him in his heart. He was simply a dumbstruck fool. He forced himself to think of William Simson to erase any longing in his features.

"I cannot discount the notion, but it might have been a fluke, something as simple as bad meat."

She nodded, her expression grim. Inhaling deeply, she said, "Matthew, about last night—"

He cut her off. He needed to take charge of the conversation because if he let her lead, he had the feeling she could and would control his every move.

He bit out the lie. "I think it best if we avoid each other, Alex." Fight with me, he silently ordered. *Realize that I am not the man for you.*

Hoping for more reaction than the blank stare she wore, he asked, "Well? Have you nothing to say?"

"Oh," she replied, smiling tightly, "there's plenty I have to say to you."

"As in?" Matthew demanded.

Alex bit her cheek, biding her time, letting him wait it out. Oh, how he made her want to resort to violence. Not look her in the eye, will he? Well, he'd just have to pay for that little bit of rudeness.

Who did he think he was fooling? Did he think that by acting standoffish and sequestering his emotions that she would just let her feelings for him go? Oh, no. Every move he made, in fact, she saw in a different light. By avoiding her eyes, he only served to reinforce what she already knew. He had feelings for her; he didn't want her to know about them; and he wasn't planning on sharing them with her any time soon.

She'd see about that.

"Alex?"

She met his cool gray gaze. "Yes?" She was not going to give him more than that. Let him come to me, she thought.

Rewarded by him raking a hand over his face and through his hair, she waited.

"We need to set boundaries," he insisted.

"Distance, you mean."

"Exactly."

He looked relieved, she thought. How foolish of him. She leaned forward. "And why is that?"

He leaned back, pressing himself into his worn leather chair as if he wished to become part of its design.

"Why?"

"Yes. Why? Does your vocabulary not include that word?"

"Alex—"

His voice rose and she smiled. She had come to recognize it was an internal defense on his part. The louder he became, the more she knew she was getting to him.

"Why are you smiling?"

"You might want to think about lowering your voice, Matthew," she said quietly, gently.

He propped his elbows on the desk and sank his head into his hands. He murmured something unintelligible under his breath.

She continued on in a voice suited to afternoon tea, not the most important conversation of her life. "You ought to lower your voice because people might find us alone." She leaned in, whispered, "And make *assumptions*."

His eyes lit with frustration. "You are an insufferable, insufferable woman," he said with the emotion of a man just having been sent to the gallows.

"So I've been told. Several times," she said, taking no offense.

He muttered, running his hands over his face. "Where were we?" he asked, looking rather unglued.

"Distance," she provided cheerfully and he scowled.

Raising her gaze, she stared at him. The gray of his eyes had darkened, looking almost black. His anger should have frightened her, but it didn't. She saw beneath it a man who unwittingly revealed more than he wanted and was angry with himself for it.

He stood and paced the room. She rose from her seat.

Taking a step forward, toward him, she tilted her head slightly to look him in the eye. Her height, she suddenly decided, she would never curse again. She slipped her hand into his hair. Woodenly, he didn't even blink.

With the pad of her thumb, she traced his lower lip and felt a slight loosening of his shoulders. His hands gripped her upper arms, but tenderly, no pressure.

His head dropped in defeat. "Why don't I frighten you?" he whispered. "I'm a hard man, too callused by life to be any good to anyone. Especially you."

She ran a finger along his cheek, down to his chin, resting it in his dimple. "You would never hurt me."

"How? How do you know?"

She broke free of his grasp and lifted her hand, placing it on the soft blue cotton of his shirt, covering his chest. She felt his heart pounding beneath her palm. "Because of what's in here." She lifted his hand and placed it over her heart, which beat slightly faster than usual. "And in here."

"No."

The word was rough, emotion choking it as he spoke.

She arched her eyebrows. "Yes."

"Stubborn *and* insufferable," he whispered, before pulling her to him, holding her, rocking her.

Suddenly, he jerked backward, putting a good three feet of distance between them. "No," was all he said.

She shook her head, disbelieving. The stubborn, stubborn man! Why, she asked herself, did he continually pull away? What wound in his past still festered? And why couldn't he see that she was the balm he needed? It was so painfully obvious to her.

Standing firm despite the overwhelming desire to sink into the nearest chair, she said, "You continue to deny yourself. Why, Matthew?" Her voice was low. Husky. She scarcely recognized it.

"You don't know me," he said roughly.

"I know enough."

He pressed his eyes closed, opened them quickly. "I am not the man for you. Kissing you will not change that fact, loving you will not change that fact."

Did he just admit he loved her? She didn't dare hope, not when he continually pushed her away, so she pressed on. "Why aren't you the man for me?" she persisted.

"Because I'm not!" he shouted.

"Yelling, Matthew, will not make it so."

"Go, Alex." He pushed a hand through his hair. "Please, just go."

"I'll go, but I'm not giving up, Matthew."

"The bond you seek will never happen between us."

Shaking her head forcefully, she said, "I refuse to believe that's true." Hating herself for the tears she heard in her voice, she continued. "You are the first man that ever made me feel beautiful." She tilted her head, smiled slightly, fingering the tears gathering in her eyes. "You're the first man who ever saw past the too-long legs, the plain brown eyes, the dull hair. You're the first man," she said with a catch in her voice, "to make me feel desirable." She wiped at the moisture that had leaked out of her eyes. "You, Matthew, are the first man with whom I ever imagined spending my life."

He opened his mouth, but she held up a hand to silence him.

"I don't know how it happened, how this love started to grow. There's something between us that can't be denied, no matter how hard you try to ignore it. Yes, I could walk away, leave you to run the *Amazing Grace*. I could let you slip out of my life forever. But I won't. My father raised me to be strong. To fight for what I believe." She watched him, his mask of hardness slipping. "Matthew," she said slowly, "I believe in you."

"You shouldn't." His voice turned hoarse. "I've done things . . ."

She shook her head. "What happened in your past stays in the past. I won't give up on us. Not now. Not ever. I suggest," she said, taking a deep breath, "that you stop fighting me."

He pushed his hands deep into his pockets. "You are my wife and I vowed to take care of you, to protect you." His voice caught. "Don't you see that by keeping you away, I'm fulfilling that vow?"

Biting back a smile, she noted the effort it took for him to speak those words. "No, Matthew," she said firmly. "You are protecting yourself. From hurt, I suppose." The wind rattled the porthole window. "Who was it that left you before, left this pain in you so deep, you feel you can't love another? Your mother?"

Silence held rein between the two. Finally, he said, "How can you be so sure it would work between the two of us?"

She recognized that he didn't answer her question, but didn't press. Softly, she said, "Because I know . . ."

He took another step back, toward the window. The afternoon light faded into a soft glow. "Know what?"

She took a deep breath. This whole conversation had been a gamble, one, she felt, she had won. "I know that you love me."

She watched his eyes widen, then narrow on her face.

Before he could speak, to deny, she said, "I love you too, Matthew."

He swallowed, visibly pained. "Please, Alex. Don't. Don't love me."

"I already do."

"I'm not worthy of your love."

"Why ever not? Because of your past?"

Turning around to face her, he shouted, "I keep telling you. I'm not a good person."

Tipping her head, she said lightly, "No?"

"Stop being so playful! This is serious. I'm not nice. I'm mean." He growled for effect, nearly making her giggle. He added, solemnly, "I have a temper."

"So I've noticed, but it's all a bluff to protect yourself. Your heart is good."

"No, it's not. It's horrible," he pointed out. "Black, even."

She bit back a laugh. "It's good. I'm not saying it doesn't have a few weaknesses, but whose doesn't?" She took a step toward the door, placed her hand on the knob.

"I don't suppose you'll keep your distance?" he asked hopefully.

"From my husband?" she asked, shocked. "What will people say?"

"Alex?"

"You said in name only. A marriage," he clarified. "I don't want to hurt you."

"You won't."

"But you said . . ."

"I lied, Matthew. There's nothing I would like more than to be your wife." Her cheeks heated, but she forced herself to say the words. "In every way."

She dashed from the room before he had a chance to

reply. Hurrying down the enclosed hallway, she ran down the steps to the Hurricane Deck as quickly as she could.

It was a risk, walking away when she did. He needed time to absorb all she told him, without painfully detailing each of his supposed faults.

She smiled. In a way it was so sweet how he tried to protect her. As if she needed protecting from his love. She'd wait for him to realize that by denying her his love, he was hurting her more than his protecting her from it ever would.

Breathing hard, she tried to catch her breath by pausing in the enclosed corridor of the Texas Deck when she heard footsteps rushing after her.

Walking quickly, she pushed through the door into the fading sunshine, hoping to avoid another pointless argument with her husband.

She was making her way to the starboard side of the ship, completing a loop, when the footsteps caught up to her.

She stopped, whirled around to face him when suddenly a blinding pain exploded through her head. Nausea coiled into a tight spring in her stomach and stars danced before her eyes just as complete darkness blinded her. She tried to scream out as she felt herself being lifted and dropped over the railing, but no sound emerged from her frightened lips.

Chapter Thirteen

"Alex."

She heard her name whispered. Someone gently rubbed her cheeks. She moaned, coughed, gagged. Pain ripped through her head. Nausea roiled up her throat.

"Water," she rasped. She wanted to open her eyes, but the throbbing was too intense. She wanted to sleep, but again, the pain would not allow her to fall back into the oblivion from which she had emerged.

She could hear motion in the room. The shuffling of feet, a door opening and closing, the rustle of clothing.

"Matthew?" she asked, tentatively.

"I'm here, sweet."

The mattress dipped and she knew he had sat down next to her. He took her hand, held it tightly.

His skin felt hot. Scorching hot on hers before she realized she was freezing. Her teeth began to chatter. The warmth from Matthew's hand disappeared and she felt the weight of another blanket being placed on top of her.

Alex tried to open her eyes, managed a thin slit, but the light of the room seemed blinding and she quickly slammed her lids shut. "What happened to me?"

"You took a little swim," he offered.

"I don't—" It took all her effort to think of the words she wanted to say, and it completely drained her to speak them. "Can't swim."

"I am quite aware of that." There was unmistakable humor in his voice. "Can you open your eyes?"

She tried to respond, to answer his question, but when she opened her mouth no words came out.

"Shh," he soothed. "Rest now. You took quite a blow to the head."

Again she tried to open her eyes. Squinting, her vision blurred, her lids burned. Giving up, she closed them.

"Man," Alex bit out. "It was a man." Despite the pain, she forced open her eyes, blinking against the shooting stars and blinding light.

His voice was urgent. "Did you recognize him?"

"No face." She reached up, felt the bump on her forehead. She winced. "Too fast. I turned around, saw a shadow . . . That's all I remember. Big shadow." She bit the words out, slowly.

She tried to sit up and failed as pain ruled her movements. Pressing her head into the pillow, her world went black once again.

It had turned dark. The light was on, but the room was shadowed and quiet. Very quiet, yet she sensed she wasn't alone.

"You're awake," Matthew said softly.

She turned her head, regretted the movement as pain splintered into a dozen branches across her forehead. Moaning softly, she rubbed her temples.

He rose from the chair, sat down on the edge of the bed. Reaching up, he lowered her hands and placed his fingers on her temples, rubbing in soothing circles.

Alex watched him, his eyes. Gone was the hardness, but in them was an emotion she couldn't identify.

"I didn't see his face." It was easier to talk now. The pain ebbed as long as she didn't move her head. "The man who hit me, I mean."

"What do you remember?"

His fingers felt heavenly. They managed to ease away her headache and incite a delicious sense of comfort within her at the same time.

"I had just left you when I heard footsteps. I thought it was you . . . But I didn't want to speak to you. I thought that we needed time apart. I wanted you to have time to think about what I said to you."

"That you love me." He said it gruffly, with great emotion underlying the words. It tore at her heart, made it swell. "That you want a real marriage."

"Yes."

She told him what she remembered. One of his hands continued circling the sensitive skin next to her right eye, but his right hand moved lower to caress her cheek.

"I *had been* following behind you; I wasn't finished with our conversation, but I lost sight of you," he said, picking up her story. "I had just about given up on finding you when I heard a splash. A loud splash. I looked over the starboard railing and saw you floating face down in the water. Your hair," he said weakly, wrapping strands of dark curls around his fist. "It was floating around your head as though it were a halo." His free hand waved as though he were smoothing a canvas with his palm.

Her throat tightened. Tears built in her eyes. "You saved me."

"You knew I would. I called for help and jumped in. Thank heaven I was in time." He touched her carefully over the goose's egg that had formed on her forehead.

The air in the room seemed to evaporate as the gray in his eyes lightened. It was a look she had seen only once before when he thought he was dreaming, the night of the fire. It was the look that told her he loved her without any words. It was the look that told her he was a good man, despite his many protests to the contrary. His eyes were eloquent when he chose to let his emotions show through.

"Now will you learn to swim?"

"I'll think about it," she said softly.

He ran a finger down her defiant chin as she lifted it into the air. "You scared me, honey."

She nodded, her chin bobbing, her eyes welling. "I scared me, too."

Thankfully, he dropped the idea of swimming lessons. He said, "About your attack . . . Nothing else you remember?"

She thought back to the moment she spun to face the pursuer she thought was Matthew.

"I felt . . . Oh, this is silly."

"Nothing's silly." His hand gently scraped across her face, his fingers dragging over her smooth skin.

She sought his eyes. "There was a time with Simson when I was afraid. I threatened him with a fireplace poker."

Matthew's hand stopped its caresses and balled into a

fist. She wondered if he even realized he had stopped touching her.

"There's an awareness," she continued on, "when I was with him that he is evil. I felt that apprehension when I saw the man's shadow."

"You think it was Simson?"

"No." She almost shook her head, but thought better of it. "The man was too tall. Your height, maybe Cal's."

"Not Simson."

"You sound disappointed." She struggled to sit up, and he lifted her gently, propping her against her pillows.

After several moments of silence, Matthew said, "Perhaps we should stop at the nearest dock, tie up for a few days. We can search the rooms, make sure that Simson, or one of his men, is not hiding aboard."

If they stopped for a few days, they'd never reach New Orleans in time to uphold their contract. The *Amazing Grace* would be a laughingstock and the boat's reputation ruined.

She leaned forward. "We can't miss our deadline."

"Because of buying back your house?"

Actually, she hadn't even thought about the house. Why? It had been so important to her only days before. It was Matthew, she decided. She loved him, and she didn't want to leave him. Yes, she wanted the house to remain in the family, but her place was with her husband, despite his feelings on the matter.

What did he think of her confession of love? He had yet to say, and the longer he remained silent, the more her hopes ebbed.

She fell back against the pillow fighting a headache of an altogether different sort.

"All right," he said without waiting for her answer. "We'll press on."

Out the window, stars twinkled in the dark sky, but no moon was visible from where she lay. "What time is it?"

"Nine. I'll let you rest now. I want to review the course for tomorrow. Shall I send in Lou or Jack?"

"No. I'm just going to sleep."

"I won't be long," he said, stooping to kiss her forehead, then, softly, her lips.

Enjoying the feel of his lips on hers, she smiled as she watched him walk to the door. "Why," she said with a wry smile, "that was almost husbandly."

"Yes, it was, wasn't it?" he said as he quickly ducked out the door.

Dare she hope? He hadn't exactly said the words, but he hadn't denied his feelings, either. It was more than she could have hoped for just a few days ago.

She rolled, disturbing her goose egg. She winced. Why had she felt Simson's presence when she was hit? It was impossible. Of course, she thought, laughing to herself, he could have disguised himself as one of the hogs and fit right in on the cargo deck. She smiled at the image as she felt herself drifting off into sleep.

Chapter Fourteen

"Where are we going, Matthew?" Alex asked as he led her down the dusty main street of a quaint old town. The steamboat was docked at a small landing, and he had explained that he felt safer having the boat searched for stowaways, fearing as they neared New Orleans, another tragedy would befall them. The delay would be minimal—only several hours. Hours with which they had decided to spend together exploring the cozy little town.

It had been over two days since her attack—two days which she had spent, under orders from Matthew, in bed, recovering from a slight fever. She had yet to gain another admission of love from her husband, despite her many attempts. It was downright infuriating.

"You'll see," he answered vaguely as they passed a saloon, a hotel, a small restaurant, and several charming boutiques, keeping tight hold of her hand.

After rolling her eyes, Alex glanced around. It was so

different here than back home in River Glen. This town didn't have paved streets or electric lighting. Gaslights hung from nearby businesses, their lamps unlit during the day.

Using the gloved tip of her finger, she wiped the dust out of her eye. Although it had rained farther up the river, it seemed as though this dusty little town had not seen a drop of it for quite some time.

She and Matthew stepped off the wooden sidewalk onto a narrow pathway that ran behind the town's bank.

"That saloon doesn't have gambling, does it?" She cast a wary glance back at the building that stood two stories high, decking accenting the second floor.

"Most do, Alex."

The path narrowed even more. They were pressed tightly against one another. "Does that one?"

"Most likely."

Alex stopped in her tracks. "I must go back."

Matthew took a firm hold on her arm. "No you don't."

"You don't understand," she said, trying to free her arm. It was like trying to free a piece of wood from a steel vice. Giving up, she let her arm hang limp in his grasp.

She could still see the roof of the saloon looming above the roof of the bank. A building that big would surely catch Jack's eye—which was assuming she wasn't looking for it in the first place.

"Jack's in good hands with Cal," he said as if reading her mind.

Alex looked over her shoulder at the saloon's roof, wanting to believe him. "Cal *is* trustworthy, right?"

"Absolutely."

Alex sighed. "I think Jack likes him."

"I believe the feeling is mutual."

"Do you really think so?"

He nodded. "Cal is a complicated man, though. His family—" He shook his head. "If it was meant to be, it will be."

Smiling, he wrapped her in his arms. "Come with me, Alex. Stop worrying for a day. Let's relax and have some fun together."

Looking into his eyes, she saw something she had never seen before: happiness. He wanted to be with her, to share an afternoon alone with *her.*

Biting the edge of her lip, she returned his embrace, then released him. This afternoon together would be a great opportunity to get to know her husband better. She realized how inane that sounded and laughed to herself.

"Lead on, Captain."

As he walked ahead of her, she wondered how to delve into his past without his realizing it.

Where was his father? Where did he grow up? Did he enjoy reading? Have brothers and sisters? There was so much she didn't know and yet so much she did.

She knew he had much to give in the way of love. He denied it, telling her he was unworthy of her feelings, but denying it wouldn't make it so. He had tried to push her away more than once, yet now he was taking her in his arms, laughing, teasing. Had he finally made a decision regarding their future?

The question itself scared her. Not because she was afraid of what lay ahead for them . . . No, it was because she was terrified of a life without him in it. She loved him with all her heart, past or no past. What did she care where he grew up? He was with her now and she was not going to let him go. It was as simple as that. They belonged together. She felt it all the way down to the bottom of her soul.

The path widened as it opened into a field surrounded by high rocks the color of the setting sun: orange streaked with gold and a tinge of red.

"Careful now," Matthew warned, picking his way over sharp, jagged edges.

She let go of his hand so she could use hers for balance as she crept over the outcropping of rocks. On firm ground once again, Matthew led her down a winding path, marked with a layer of fine gravel and overgrown bushes.

"Where are you taking me?"

"Just a little farther," he answered evasively.

She looked around curiously. "What is this place?"

"A quarry."

"A quarry? As in blasting rock for bricks and cobblestone and building materials quarry?"

"The very same."

Her voice rose. "Why are we here, Matthew?" Her suspicion mounted. Although they didn't have one in River Glen, she knew quarries were popular places to—

"Swimming lessons." He stopped as he reached the end of the path and with a grand flourish presented her with a swimming hole.

Backing up the path, she said, "Oh, no. Out of the question."

Grabbing hold of her hand, he pulled her into the clearing. "You have to learn how to swim, Alex. I would've thought what happened to you two days ago would prove so beyond doubt."

"You would have thought wrong," she said in a voice that was close to a whine. She cleared her throat.

"You need to learn."

Steeling herself against the tender pleading in his eyes, she bit out, "No, I don't. You rescued me. You'll do it again if the need ever arises."

"What if I'm not there?"

"I'll drown," she said defiantly, crossing her arms.

"You're being childish. Why are you so afraid of the water?"

"I'm not afraid of the water!"

Why couldn't he leave well enough alone? Deep down she knew she needed to learn to swim. If she was going to make a life for herself on the river it was a basic need. If it had only been dark out . . . Unfortunately, the sun was high, bright, and she remained childishly stubborn.

Actually, her fear was based in childhood, of children laughing at her long legs, bony torso. Arms too long, neck too high. She looked quite like a giraffe, truth be told.

"What is it then? Why are you scared?"

Ignoring the soothing timbre of his voice, Alex sat down on a huge boulder.

"Alex?"

She heard the impatience in his voice, didn't care. She wasn't budging from her spot on the rock. "I'm not going in, Matthew."

"Yes, you are. I am not going to risk losing you again. Once was enough to age me twenty years."

Snapping her head up, she looked at him to gauge his sincerity. He was telling the truth. She saw it in his eyes, in the set of his jaw.

"It's too cold," she protested lamely.

"It's beautiful."

"I . . . I have a headache," she said, moaning and touching the lump on her head.

Out of the corner of her eye, she watched his mouth

harden into a thin line. Determining that she had pushed him too far, she made a run for the path. She completed only two steps.

"You move pretty fast for someone who's in so much pain," he mocked, holding her tightly around her waist.

She kicked her legs, wiggled to be free, but he kept a firm hold on her. "Put me down," she shrieked.

"You can either go into the water by your own free will, or I can throw you in, you insufferable woman," he offered in a controlled voice rich with humor.

Pushing at his arms, she said, "Oh, you would like that, wouldn't you?"

"Immensely."

She panicked as he inched closer and closer to the water. "Fine!"

He lowered her so that her feet touched the ground. She backed away from him, smoothing the front of her blouse.

"No running."

"No running," she agreed. He didn't say anything about skipping, though. Or, perhaps, galloping. Eyeing the path, she thought about it, but decided he would catch her quickly and pitch her into the quarry, the infuriating man that he was.

"I won't look when you remove your clothes," he said. "If that's why you're afraid."

Color rose into her cheeks, heating them as easily as the temperature of a summer day.

"I won't take advantage of you, Alex. I promise."

"Pity," she mumbled.

"Pardon?"

"Nothing," she snapped.

"You can change behind that rock." He pointed to a large boulder.

Once behind the rock, she pressed her back against it. Again, she thought about fleeing.

"Don't even think about running," he warned from nearby.

"I won't." She was grateful he couldn't see her left eye blinking. She was simply biding her time to make her escape.

"I'll catch you if you do and then, Splash!"

She believed him. "You're a horrible man!" she called out.

"So I've been telling you," he countered.

"Well, I'm beginning to believe it," she said with fake sweetness and frowned when he laughed.

She unbuttoned her blouse, peeling it over her shoulders.

"What's taking so long, Alex?" he called out.

"You've obviously never seen a woman undress, Captain. We have layers to remove."

Stalling for time, she made rustling noises. She looked down at herself, at her thin undershirt and knickers. It did little to hide her gangliness. This proved to be one of the few times she wished she wore dresses. At least then she'd have petticoats to hide behind.

He was her husband, she reminded herself. "Don't look until I tell you," she ordered.

His laughter echoed through the quarry, bouncing off the rocks, reverberating through her. "Yes, madam!"

Creeping out from behind her hiding place, she ran to the water's edge. Taking a glance over her shoulder, she saw Matthew at the edge of the woods, keeping his word by looking away. Shockingly cold, the water stole her breath as she stepped into it, but she was determined to see this through.

She waded in to her knees, her little clothing becoming

saturated and horrifyingly clingy, though thankfully not see-through since the fabrics were dark. She sank down as the murky water reached her waist, determined that she was in deep enough. The dark water covered her up to her shoulders as she knelt down, her floating hair tickling her neck.

"I'm—" She cleared her throat to erase the quiver and tried again. "I'm ready," she called out.

"It's about time," he complained, walking toward the water. At the edge, he kicked off his shoes and removed his socks.

She watched with growing anticipation as he unbuttoned his shirt. Was it her imagination or was the act innately intimate? His hands paused on each button, pushing it through its hole. Her gaze never left his body.

Lowering his hands, he unbuttoned his pants, slid them down his legs, revealing long underwear. He stepped into the water with them on and she felt oddly disappointed with his modesty.

The water rippled as he made his way closer to her. "You're shivering," he remarked, touching his hand to her trembling chin.

"I think we should probably start out in a deeper part of the quarry," he suggested as ripples gently lapped at his stomach.

"I'd rather stay here."

Arching an eyebrow, he regarded her carefully. "It will be easier out there."

"I'm up to my neck now as it is," she reasoned.

"No. You're up to your waist; I believe you're sitting down."

She growled. "Fine."

Matthew had continued on, giving her instructions about

floating as she waded deeper, never revealing herself. When the water had reached Matthew's ribcage Alex deemed that it was more than deep enough.

"Are you paying attention?" he asked her.

Lifting her head, she found him staring at her. "No," she answered honestly.

He sighed. "Why don't you stand up, and we'll start with learning how to float? Even if it's the only thing you learn, it can save your . . . Holy Mother," he whispered, looking up at the sky as she rose out of the water. Her dark shirt molded her like a second skin.

He stepped in front of her as if someone might see. She watched as he pushed a hand through his hair, and she waited, her lips trembling, not from fear, but from withholding tears. Did he think her horrible?

He didn't say anything. His gaze dropped to her face and he stared at her as though she were an act in a traveling circus. She sank back down in the water, feeling exposed and simply dreadful. She had known this would happen!

Matthew sank down with her. It was then that she noticed the change in his eyes. The cold she felt seeped quickly away as the desire in his gaze warmed her skin, her heart.

"You are so beautiful."

"I'm not. My waist . . . my legs . . ." Her voice drifted off.

"Do you own a looking glass, Alex?"

The way he said her name made her throat tighten. So softly, barely audible. Almost as if he was afraid to say it aloud.

"Yes."

His shoulders were broad, well muscled. They stiffened as she rested her head against his chest.

"Can you not see that you are beautiful?" he asked, ever so quietly.

"No, I cannot. My hair is the color of mud. My eyes, the color of mud when it dries. My limbs are long—"

He cut her off. "I see a beautiful woman with amazing brown eyes that convey emotion better than words. I see hair that a man can lose himself in and would be grateful if never found. I see lips that are sweeter than any sugar; a neck that is long and graceful which simply begs for a man's lips to be upon it; hands that are gentle, soothing."

She could only stare at him, mouth agape. His words were ones she never thought she'd hear. The emotion of it all choked back any response she might have had.

"I'm a complex man, Alex," he murmured, kissing her nose, her cheeks, her neck.

She laughed. "As if I didn't know."

"You make me want to be the person you see in me."

She cupped his cheek and looked into his eyes. "You already are. You're my husband, Matthew. I shall never love another."

He cupped her face which was only inches from hers and stared intently into her eyes. "You know what you are saying?"

"Forever, Matthew. Forever. My husband."

More than anything he wanted to be her husband, to be the father of her children.

She was telling him it was all within his reach.

If he chose to take it.

He looked deeply into her eyes. Love burst forth from her rich brown gaze. It humbled him, her love that she so freely gave. What was it that she saw in him that he could not see for himself?

Her lips parted as if she was going to say something, but she said nothing. They stood, chest deep, in the cold water making the most monumental decision to be made.

He couldn't change the past, he knew that now. But he could have a future. A future with a woman who loved him. With a woman he loved more than he thought a man capable.

The water pulsed around his chest as she slipped her fingers into his hair. He noticed she was careful not to touch the fuzz of hair that covered the scar on his head. She twined her fingers through the locks at his neck and tugged gently to get his attention. Through a haze of indecision, he looked at her.

"I love you, Matthew. You. Not who you may have been, or who you may become. You. Please, please, stop thinking and start feeling."

Her eyes were his undoing. He could get lost in her chocolate orbs. How easily she expressed what she was feeling with only one look.

Wrapping his arms around her, he pulled her to him, gently capturing her mouth.

"I won't let you go," he said between kisses.

"You don't have to."

He kissed her then, sealing the bond between them as surely as if they had spoken vows. Her kisses were intoxicating. The first time they had kissed his knees had gone weak. He felt the same way now.

He cupped her chin, holding her tightly. He pulled his mouth from hers and was just about to tell her that he loved her when he heard a loud whistle closely followed by another whistle. A steamboat's whistle.

"Isn't that the *Amazing Grace*?"

"Something's wrong," he said, grabbing her arm, pulling her out of the water.

Another whistle, longer.

On land, he stopped, gave her a quick kiss after scanning her from head to toe. "Beautiful. Hurry, go get dressed." Why was it whenever they got close enough to really share their feelings, their passion, it was interrupted?

Another whistle pulled him out of his thoughts of fate and her fickle ways.

At least there was a whistle, he reasoned. That meant that the steamer was still floating. What could have gone wrong? He slipped his pants on which became damp as he pulled them up his legs.

Alex appeared from behind the boulder, fastening the buttons on her shirt. She sat on the ground and pulled on her boots.

"What do you think it is?"

"Not sure."

"Do you think it's bad?"

He shoved his foot into his shoe. "Yes."

She stood, wiping her hands on her pants. He took hold of her elbow and helped her up the path and over the rocks. He caught her as she slipped, nearly tumbling down a slope of jagged rock, but she didn't pause. Her rush to get back to the *Amazing Grace* was as great as his own.

As they crested the hill, he saw the street that had been empty only an hour before was now filled with hundreds of black and white spotted squealing hogs.

"Oh, no!"

He stopped, dumbstruck by the sight. His crewmembers were trying their best to round up the hogs, but there were too many. Locals were not helping; instead they hustled the hogs off to their homes, and one fellow was even loading them into a wagon. Matt counted five hogs alone in that man's possession.

"We have to get them back!" Alex yelled, surging into the fray.

He reached for her, but missed as she ran into the street, trying to catch hold of one of the hogs. He ran after her, but she was already sucked into the rush. He ran down the wooden sidewalk, past the people laughing at the scene. Near the saloon, he saw Jack and Cal using ropes to lasso hogs, then handing them over to Jonah. Lou stood on the stage, ushering returning hogs back into the cargo hold where they were being returned to their pens.

He spun, returning to the main street of the town. He helped round up the hogs, as many as he and the crew could. It was tiring, hot, hard work. It was two hours before there were no more hogs wandering the streets.

Alex stepped up behind him, covered from head to toe in caked mud. Her hair had dried into a clump of muck, and he suddenly realized he looked no better. They climbed the stage together.

Her grim expression tore at him. "How many did we lose?"

"Not sure yet."

The hogs aboard squealed in protest. "Think they're singing the praises of freedom?" Lou shouted as they approached them.

"No doubt," Jack said as she and Cal came up behind them.

"Any count, yet?" Matt had to yell over the deafening din. He ordered slop to be brought in and soon the hogs were silently eating.

"Captain?" Jonah called out.

"Yes?"

"Two hundred forty-four."

Matt nodded his thanks.

"Two hundred forty-four? Hogs?" Alex asked with a squeak in her voice.

"Yes."

She started toward the stage in a hurry.

He grabbed her arm. "Where are you going?"

"We need to get them back, Matthew."

"We just can't go out there and raid people's farms."

"Why not!" she demanded. "They're ours. Without those hogs, the *Amazing Grace's* reputation will forever be sullied."

"We need to think about this," he announced. "Formulate a plan."

The sun had nearly finished its descent, the last streaks of light casting shadows on the sandy banks, the water, on the small town she no longer thought quaint.

She and Matthew were in his office, having already cleaned up. They were waiting for Cal, Jack, and Lou to arrive.

Patiently, she waited for him to say something, to reveal this plan of his, but apparently he was waiting for the others to join them.

Alex longed to speak of what happened at the quarry, but the hogs, or lack thereof, weighed on her mind. She and Matthew would have time enough to speak of their promises to each other.

She stole a peek at him as he pored over the ledgers on his desk. His brow furrowed, his mouth was grim as he scratched figures on a piece of scrap paper.

Refusing to believe the *Amazing Grace* would not succeed, she kept her gaze focused out the window on a bird perched on a snag sticking out of the water.

It was a beautiful bird. Small, yet graceful. She jumped as Matthew placed a hand on her shoulder. The bird flew away.

"Alex?"

She turned to face him, surprised to find him standing just behind her. Compassion lit his eyes. She threw herself into his arms and let him hold her. She felt so secure in his arms. As if the world couldn't intrude on her happiness. Out of his arms, she felt as though everything was falling apart.

Tucking a loose curl behind her ear, he released her.

"Together, we'll get through this," she said, but her tears threatened the truth of her words.

He held her closer. "Such faith. How?"

This she could talk about, because she believed in their relationship so fiercely. "I knew we were meant to be together the moment you touched me at my father's service." She looked up at him and smiled. "Such a small touch." Using the tip of her finger, she brushed the area of her wrist Matthew had touched the day she buried her father. "Yet I knew. There was something between us, even then." Gazing at him, and noting the darkening of his gray eyes, she asked, "Did you feel it?"

"Yes. I hadn't known you knew it was me." The words came out in a rough purr. "And I see now that you are right. We'll get through this together."

Alex smiled, wide and bright. "As husband and wife?"

He cupped her chin. "I believe I told you that I'm never letting you go."

Reaching out, she grasped his chin and brought it to her mouth for a kiss. Moments later, she released him, feeling weak and unsatisfied. "And I told you that you didn't have to let me go."

"Then it's settled." A shadow crept over his eyes. "However, there are some things I need to tell you as soon as we have more time."

What was hiding in that shadow? She pushed away her concerns. They would talk. What was important was that they had each other.

"Come in," Matthew yelled when a knock sounded.

Lou, Jack, and Cal came into the room. Cal took a seat at the desk. After placing a pair of reading glasses on, he took a peek at the ledger and frowned. "By the looks of this, you and I have arrived at the same solution."

"Come to share it with us, gentlemen?" Jack asked.

Matthew motioned to Cal to explain. He said, "I think the only way we can get all the hogs back is to buy them back."

Alex gasped. "Buy back our own hogs? How ridiculous!"

"Alex," Cal said, "these people aren't going to hand them over with a 'Sorry, ma'am.' They own those hogs now, whether we like it or not."

She turned to Matthew. "That's not fair!"

Before he could respond, Cal said, "Matt, when will you get the insurance check for the *Muddy Waters*?"

"Not for a few more weeks at least. I have money enough at a bank in New Orleans, but there isn't nearly enough time to have it wired north in time to keep our schedule."

"I have some money," Jack offered.

Alex turned toward her, surprised, as Matthew said, "How much?"

"About a thousand."

"Where on earth did you get that kind of mon—" Alex

broke off her sentence. "Do not answer; I don't want to know."

"Still not enough," Cal said, tapping the pencil on the desk.

"I have about a thousand on hand in the safe," Matthew said. "The rest I sunk into the *Amazing Grace*, preparing her for her trip."

"How much more do we need?" Lou asked.

Matthew said, "About two thousand, I would guess."

Alex felt hope dry up inside of her. Two thousand more? Good heavens. Silence settled on the room as daylight fell into dusk. Matthew turned on a light and a warm glow filled the room.

Cal cleared his throat. "There is one other person who can give us the money."

"Who?" they all asked in unison.

"Myself."

"You?" Matthew asked, clearly shocked, his untamed eyebrows burrowing into a deep V.

All eyes were riveted on Cal's face. He looked down, obviously embarrassed by the attention if the red staining of his face was any indication.

"I have some money saved."

"But you need that—" Matthew began.

"You can repay me when you get your insurance check."

Alex watched, feeling helpless. She couldn't take Cal's money. It was too much, too much generosity. And for Matthew to use his insurance money? She shook her head. She couldn't allow it. "No," Alex stated without further hesitation.

She looked to Matthew, who stared at her in concern. "It's too much," she said, pleading with him to understand.

His gray eyes softened. He dipped his head, whispered

into her ear. His breath tickled her ear, his words warmed her heart. "You're my wife. What's mine is yours."

Tears stung her eyes. His loving gaze never wavered. Finally, she nodded her approval.

Once he had her approval, Cal said, "Tonight we will draft a notice to let the townsfolk know that we are looking to buy some hogs and post it first thing in the morning."

Chapter Fifteen

Unable to sleep, Matt lay on his side, the blankets tucked between his legs. By all rights he should have been fast asleep, but matters weighed heavily on his mind, his heart.

A thin sliver of moonlight spilled into the room, lighting a small vein of the threadbare rug. He had watched over the past hour as the vein of light slowly eased its way toward the left. Soon, it would climb the wall and disappear as the moon began its descent.

His heart warmed at Alex's rhythmic breathing. He looked over to the bed where she lay sleeping and smiled at the image she made, completely wrapped in blankets like an Egyptian mummy.

She had protested when he opted to sleep on the couch, and hadn't been pleased when he refused to tell her why he didn't want to share her bed. Even now, he wondered if his old-fashioned notions were as foolish as they sounded. But he was adamant.

He wouldn't sleep in their bed until they were properly married. When he had taken his vows, he hadn't really meant them, hadn't taken them as seriously as he should have. It was something he wanted to rectify as soon as possible. He wanted a real wedding, with real emotion . . . Only then would he go to her as her husband.

Flipping onto his back, he pulled at his thin blanket. He never needed much more to cover him, even in the dead of winter. If he was chilled, he would put on a pair of long cotton underwear that covered him from neck to ankle. But tonight he was not chilled, not nearly.

Despite his vow to never let her go, he was worried that once Alex found out about his past, she might leave him. He was determined to do his best to explain why he had been driven to a life of crime, but his explanations sounded hollow, even to him. What would she say? How would she react?

Blinking slowly, he begged for sleep to overtake him. Just a few hours' worth. Just enough to stop the whirl of thoughts swirling in his head. But of course if he slept, he dreamed. At least the images when he was awake, he could control. Unlike the memories and nightmares that usually plagued his sleep.

His stomach clenched, and he decided to put the issue of Alex out of his mind for a while. When he thought of her, he thought solely of her, and he had other matters, as the captain of the *Amazing Grace*, to consider.

Someone was sabotaging their trip.

Who? And why?

His first, immediate thought was Simson. The odious little man had to be behind the problems plaguing the steamer. Punching the pillow behind his head, Matt rolled again, trying to find a comfortable position on the impossibly small sofa.

Simson was just the type of insane man to want complete control over others' lives. It also happened that both Matt and Alex had given him cause to dislike them. And Matt knew for a fact that William Simson wasn't one to let a grievance, imagined or otherwise, go.

Simson had to have help. It was clear after a thorough search of the boat that Simson himself was not aboard. That left a list of passengers, as well as his crew members. While he doubted one of his crewmen would betray him, he understood the lengths to which some men would go for money.

In his head, he went over the faces of his men, trying to decide which one would be most likely to betray him. Not one man came immediately to mind. They were his friends, he thought viciously, and here he was thinking one of them sold out to Simson! He couldn't believe it. Wouldn't. But had to. They were the only ones with access to the hogs.

The moonlight had shifted again, starting its descent down the wall opposite Matt.

Alex mumbled something in her sleep and he once again found himself watching her. He rose, crossed the room, and sat on the edge of the bed.

Their bed.

He smoothed her hair. She had taught him that he could have happiness and love and all the things he once thought impossible. But he knew now he couldn't hide his past from her. He had to share it with her to release the demons that lived inside his heart. Only then would he be free.

"You scare me too," he whispered, and her eyes fluttered open.

She blinked once, twice. "You heard me that night. Why didn't you stop me?"

The deeply burnished golden heart pendant she wore constantly lay nestled in the hollow of her throat above the high white lace collar of her nightgown. He traced it with the tip of his index finger. "I couldn't. I needed so badly to hear what you had to say."

His breath caught as she smiled. "Well, if it had any influence on you marrying me, then I'm glad you heard." Suddenly she frowned. "What's wrong? You seem . . . tense."

He took a deep breath and swallowed over the lump in his throat. "I need to tell you about my past, but I don't want to frighten you."

She sat up, bracing her weight on her elbows. "That look in your eye is a distant one. I'm frightened for you, not for me. You're seeing something in your past that scares you."

For years he had worked on, perfected, keeping his emotions hidden. But more than once she had seen the fear in his eyes. She had insisted he loved her when he told her he didn't. How could she know him so well?

He had sensed there was something magical between them the first day they met. He had felt it; she had felt it. He didn't know if it had a name, the intimate knowledge between two strangers. He put no faith into stories of people who had loved in past lifetimes, but he almost believed it true. How else could they know one another so completely? Perhaps he would never know why they were connected this way, but he knew as surely as he breathed that he would cherish the bond they shared.

"There's really no easy way to say this, so I'll come right out with it."

He told her of his youth, being orphaned when he was seven, of having to take to the streets, of having to steal and cheat and beg. And of having no remorse for those crimes because it was all he knew. He told her of the grime, of the awful things he had seen, of the people who had hurt him. And he told her of the river, and of the boats that had become his salvation.

He watched her closely for a reaction, but saw none in her usually easily readable eyes. She sat straight, said nothing, as she gazed at him.

"The year I turned thirteen I was sleeping in a basement room below a saloon. The barkeep, a man named Aiden, had taken me under his wing, tried to keep me out of trouble. He gave me odd jobs, food to eat, a place to sleep. He, he became my family."

"An amazing man."

Matt nodded. "Late one night I awoke to the sound of fighting." He clenched his fist. "Fighting in the saloon wasn't all that uncommon, but the saloon had been closed for hours at that point.

"I crept up the stairs and saw a man wearing a mask bent over Aiden's body. A knife stuck out of Aiden's chest."

Alex gasped.

He took a deep breath. "I—I wasn't thinking. I ran up to Aiden, tried to see if he was still breathing."

"Was he?" she whispered.

Matt shook his head. "The man who killed him knocked me down, telling me I was next if I didn't stay out of his way as he pulled the knife out of Aiden."

The night came back to him. The smell of liquor, of blood. His stomach turned. "I knew Aiden kept a loaded rifle under the bar. I crept to it as the man unloaded the safe. When he finally turned around, I took aim."

The raw rush of fear came back to him. His palms dampened. He laughed, no joy in the sound. "I told him we were going to the jail. That he was going to tell the police what he'd done."

He looked at Alex, saw the moisture in her eyes. "I didn't want to shoot him, but he came at me with the knife." He shuddered. "I fired, then I ran. I ran to the river, but there were no boats there that night. I hid in an old crate, too afraid to move. The next morning I snuck out of my cubby long enough to buy a paper. The report of Aiden's death was but a small article near the back. The police thought Aiden had managed to shoot the robber before dying. There was no investigation, but I knew what happened. I knew I was a murderer."

A tear slipped down Alex's cheek. She placed her hand on his arm. "Murderer is such a harsh word. Did you take another's life? Yes. But answer me this, Matthew," she said softly. "Would he have taken yours if you hadn't taken his?"

He jerked his hand away. "But I killed him!"

Storminess settled in her dark gaze. "Did you enjoy it, Matthew? Do you like hurting others?"

His chest tightened. "What? No, of course not."

"Then how can you compare yourself to the man that killed Aiden? He . . . he was the one who murdered."

"I should be in jail."

Tugging off the covers, she knelt in front of him. "There's not a judge in Ohio who would have convicted you, Matthew. Your actions were self-defense, nothing more than that. You were a child defending yourself. Will the hurt you feel at taking another's life ever heal? I don't know. Am I glad you did what you did?" Dark locks of hair tumbled over her shoulders. "Absolutely. Because if you hadn't, you wouldn't be here today. With me. Married to me."

She leaned forward and circled his neck with her arms. The relief that washed through him knocked the breath from his lungs. He doubled over, his head landing in her lap. She ran her fingers through his hair, comforting him as only she could.

Softly, she said, "I am so proud of the man you have become. A man who has made so much of his life, despite a childhood that could have ruined him."

"I had nightmares for years," he admitted. "I still have them."

Her expression softened. "I'd like to say they will go away, but what you experienced will likely never disappear from your thoughts."

The sliver of moonlight had disappeared. It would be morning soon. "Maybe now I can put the matter to rest."

She gently kissed his forehead. "Maybe."

"Alex?" he said, rising onto his elbows.

"Hmm?" Her fingers twisted through his hair.

With the weight of guilt ebbing from his heart, he said, "Will you marry me?"

Her face brightened, lighting his soul. "We already are married!"

He pulled in a deep breath, trying to calm the emotions swirling inside, twisting his chest into a knot. "Sweet, I want a real marriage, with vows spoken out of love and trust. I want to know that when we're standing before a man of God that we will truly be husband and wife in every sense of the word. I want to know that you will wake by my side every morning, and every night, I want to hear you read the stories you wrote for our children, and I want to know that you love me as much as I love you.

"You are my heart, Alex. I need you in my life, to keep the shadows at bay, to remind me of all the beauty in the world." He traced her cheek with his fingertip. "Say you'll marry me and be my wife, my lover, the mother of my children."

His finger caught a teardrop rolling down her cheek as she said, "My father once told me that love was a battle. Well, Matthew, I've fought long enough. I surrender. My heart surrenders. I will be honored to marry you. Again," she added with a teary smile. "All I've ever wanted was a family. A husband who loved me . . . children. To think I might someday carry your child inside of me . . . It's more than I ever imagined possible."

She stiffened ever so slightly and he found her damp eyes had turned serious. "What is it?"

"There is a problem."

He couldn't imagine anything coming between them ever again. "What?"

"My house."

He sat up, his shoulders stiff with tension. "The river is my life."

She smiled. "I know that, but that house is where I was raised. I can't bear to see it leave my family."

"You want to live there, without me?"

Rolling her eyes, she said, "And you call *me* insufferable?"

She laughed and some of the tension seeped out of his body. "What are you trying to say, Alex?"

"If it's okay with you, I would still like to go back to River Glen come summer to bid on the house. We can give it to Lou and Jack. Just so long as one of us lives there."

He kissed her forehead, settled her in his arms. "How are the summers in River Glen? Hot? Because," he teased, "I don't like not having a breeze from the water . . ." Cincinnati would never again hold power over him as it had only a month ago. No more would he feel the terror, hear the whispers of guilt on the wind when docked there. Thanks to Alex. She had opened his eyes, his heart.

She poked him in the ribs with her elbow, and he laughed. As she told him about her father, her sisters, her childhood home, and the odd town she was raised in, he leaned back, feeling for the first time, at peace. So at peace in fact, that he might, he mused, one day even teach her how to pilot the *Amazing Grace*.

Inwardly he laughed at himself. His thoughts, to his judgment, sounded suspiciously like mooning.

Chapter Sixteen

With New Orleans's busy waterfront just ahead of him, Matt stepped out onto the deck, in search of his wife.

As he approached the stage, he heard the most beautiful of lullabies being sung and followed the sound. Much to his surprise, it was Lou who was doing the singing, and quite well, he might add.

"That was beautiful," he said, stepping up to her.

She blushed and looked away.

Alex had told him she was shy about her singing, but she wasn't just shy, she was *painfully* shy. He changed the subject. "Have you seen Alex?"

"Sorry, Matt," Lou said.

Matt wiped a hand across his brow. Temperatures were unusually warm for February in New Orleans, and he was feeling the heat dressed in his suit.

The stiff black material was itchy and he longed for the soft cotton of his regular shirts, but knew prospective clients would expect a captain to be finely dressed. He tugged at the knot in his tie, scanned the empty decks. His gaze landed back on Lou, who was staring absently at the wharf where the *Amazing Grace* had docked early that morning, holding a piece of paper in her hand.

"That is the first steamboat I have seen other than ours," she said, motioning to a steamer docked farther down the wharf.

"Once this whole wharf would have been filled with steamboats."

"That one looks quite old."

"See the hoist on the wharf on the leeward side?"

"Yes."

"The steamboat's going to be taken out of the water. Dry-docked."

"Permanently?"

"I hope so."

Her innocent eyes widened. "Why is that?"

"It's one of Simson's."

Squinting against the morning sun, she stared at the steamer. "How can you tell?"

"The Simson Packet Company's colors. Blue and green."

"I am glad I've never met the dreadful man."

He grinned wryly. "I wish I could say the same."

Matt stared at the old steamer. Her colors were fading and she looked as though she favored her starboard side. Built in the 1850s, maybe '60s, he guessed.

He looked down to say his good-byes to Lou and noticed for the first time she looked ashen. She clutched the piece of paper tightly, wrinkling it.

"Are you well?" he asked.

She shook her head, her eyes brimming with tears. "A

telegraph arrived soon after we docked. It's from Mr. Nielson."

The name sounded vaguely familiar. Finally, he remembered. "Your family's solicitor?"

She nodded. With a catch in her voice, she said, "Apparently the bank auctioned the house sooner than expected. It was sold last week to an undisclosed buyer."

Matt's stomach twisted into a tight knot.

She pinned him with an unwavering violet stare. "Jack and I . . . Well, we loved our house, but without Alex there it wouldn't have been home. Buying the house back was her dream, not ours. We only went along with it because we knew how much she loved that house. How are we going to tell her? It's going to break her heart."

Matt sighed. "I'll tell her. She'll be all right once the knowledge sinks in."

"You love her, don't you?"

"Yes. Very much."

Lou dropped her chin. "It's all Jack and I ever wanted for her. I'm so very glad you came into our lives."

He crouched down, next to her. "I have been meaning to thank you," he said finally.

"For what?"

"Alex told me it was your and Jack's idea that she ask me to marry her." He looked down at the decking beneath his feet, remembering how he had first turned his wife down, and cursing himself for hurting her.

Slowly, he rose. "I'm going to look for her."

Lou's brows furrowed. "Yesterday she mentioned she planned on going into town to find some cargo to bring back to Cincinnati, but I assumed she was going with you."

"She didn't say a word to me." It would be just like her to wander off on her own. Although he loved her headstrong nature, he worried about her alone on the streets of an unknown city.

"Perhaps she took Jack."

He was shaking his head as he answered. "I just saw Jack and Cal on the Main Deck a few minutes ago."

"I don't believe she would go alone. Not with all that has happened."

"I hope you're right."

She added, "I'm glad the night passed safely."

"You and me both."

Silence lingered, and he felt uneasy. He couldn't describe why, but pricks of awareness danced down his spine. He couldn't shake the feeling that something was wrong, but couldn't pinpoint what it was exactly. Only that it had to do with Alex. Of that he was sure.

New Orleans felt like another world. Everything was so different than anything she had ever experienced. The thick air scented with spices and chicory, the architecture, the speech, mannerisms and street life. It was too much to swallow in one day.

Matthew would be proud of her accomplishments once he overcame his anger at her having gone alone. She had managed to procure a cargo of sugar cane from a plantation farther north, a shipment of seed sacks to be unloaded in Louisville, and crates of flour to be shipped north. Nary a hog—or other animal—aboard, much to her delight.

In the distance she could see the twin stacks of the *Amazing Grace* and felt an immeasurable sense of happiness. Nothing had happened during the night, and it felt as though the danger had passed since they had made it to New Orleans safely.

Now that she felt useful, garnering some of the *Amazing*

Grace's cargo, she wanted nothing more than to return to the boat and to her husband.

As she paused to cross a busy intersection, a shadow fell across her feet and she jumped back in fright. "Jonah!" Alex exclaimed, releasing her pent-up breath. "You scared me."

"Me?"

"The shadow . . ." She shook her head. "Forget it. It was nothing but my vivid imagination."

"I've been sent to find you. There's been an accident . . ."

She gasped. "Is anyone hurt?"

"I'm afraid so. The captain was tending to the boilers when a valve came loose. He's been burned terribly."

Her knees went weak beneath her, and Jonah's strong arms kept her from falling. All she could think of was Matthew. She had only just begun loving her husband—surely the fates wouldn't take him from her now!

Jonah led her to a waiting hack and helped her in. Her thoughts were all a-tumble, skittering over what little she knew about burns to the fact that she couldn't live without Matthew by her side. It took her a moment to notice that the hack was not empty as she thought it would be.

William Simson tipped his hat. "Miss Parker. Oh, it's Mrs. Kinkade now, isn't it?"

Alex shifted a horrified gaze from Jonah's face to that of William Simson's. "What . . . How?"

Simson chuckled. "The wonder of the railroad. Although I had hoped to have news of your demise by the time I reached New Orleans." He poked Jonah on the foot with his walking stick, and the young crewman yelped like a wounded puppy.

Confusion swept through her, then clarity dawned. She

turned accusing eyes to Jonah. "There was no boiler accident, was there?"

"Very perceptive of you, Alexandra." Simson smelled vaguely of cheap perfume, a scent that made her want to gag.

Slowly, her fear turned into ire. "All the destruction and undermining aboard the *Amazing Grace*—you were behind that, weren't you? You," she yelled to Jonah. Her voice caught. "You hit me and threw me into the river! And oh! The *Muddy Waters*?" she asked on a whisper. Had he blown up Matthew's steamboat, nearly killing him?

Jonah looked away from her angry glance without answering.

The carriage rolled to a stop. Jonah pushed open the door and Alex stumbled out. Both men flanked her as they led her aboard a steamboat that had seen better days.

Out of the corner of her eye she could see the *Amazing Grace* sitting proudly farther down the wharf. How long would it take before anyone noticed she was gone? How long would it be before they realized she was missing? She had to do something . . .

Suddenly she knew just what she had to do. She began to scream for help, as loudly as she was able, knowing one of the men would try to silence her. She left behind the one thing she knew Matthew would recognize as hers. Jonah clamped a hand over her mouth as he dragged her through a set of doors leading into the main deck of the old steamboat.

"You're insane!" she yelled at Simson when Jonah finally removed his sweaty palm.

"Be quiet," Jonah hissed, looking about.

"And you," she shouted at Jonah, "you're a good-for-nothing louse! Wait till Captain Kinkade hears about this!"

Simson smirked. "And how is he going to find out, Alexandra? You'll be long dead before anyone notices your absence."

Panic rose in a crashing crescendo. Alex struggled, but the two men kept tight hold of her as they forced her down a set of stairs and into the galley that smelled strongly of kerosene. Simson handed Jonah the key, instructing him to lock the door behind him and wait for his signal before opening the door again.

Fright and dread mingled with anger as she realized she was alone with him. She looked around the empty galley, at the bare counters, the large empty sink and unused ovens. There was no place to run, no place to hide. She told herself to remain calm, to think clearly as her gaze searched for an escape. Her heart pounded. There had to be a way!

Simson stood still, watching her. Goose flesh rose on her arms as fear seemed to overwhelm her other emotions.

"Jonah was amazingly easy to bribe to do my dirty work," he said boastfully. "I suppose growing up the way he did, living off the streets, the money was too easy to pass up." He laughed.

She thought of Matthew and his upbringing, how similar it was to Jonah's. Only her husband had integrity and the will to change his life, where Jonah had been weak.

Where only moments before, fear had made her a coward, thoughts of Matthew and his love for her made her strong. When Simson removed a cigar from his pocket, she took a chance and lunged for his feet, but he jumped back out of her reach, obviously seeing the attack coming.

"Now, now!" he reprimanded, lighting the cigar. Walking over to the door, he made a show of dropping the cigar into a pile of old rags. They ignited quickly, obviously the source of the kerosene she smelled.

"I'll be sure to mention Captain Kinkade's vendetta against me to the authorities when they investigate the burning of my boat. And when, and if, they find your body, I'm sure someone will come forward to claim you two had a lovers' quarrel . . . Jonah perhaps. There will be a trial, and the good captain will probably be sentenced to death. And I . . . I will collect the insurance money and buy the *Amazing Grace* from your lovely sisters."

"You're evil, vile!"

His smug expression ate at her. It was enough that he was going to kill her, but Matthew had been through so much in his life, and had lost even more at the hands of this man. Anger raged within her, reaching down into a part of her she never knew existed.

"But why?" she cried out.

His eyes narrowed and in them she saw madness. "Because I can. I always get what I want, Alexandra, and both you and that husband of yours have refused me. So now, I will simply take it. I'll be sure to give Captain Kinkade your regards," he cackled, reaching to tap on the door.

Chapter Seventeen

Matt had looked everywhere. No one in the city seemed to have seen her. She was nowhere aboard the *Amazing Grace*, either. As each moment passed that he couldn't find Alex, the more his uneasiness grew.

Simson had to be behind Alex's disappearance.

"Where would he take her?" he asked himself, pushing a hand through his hair. His stomach twisted with fear. If Simson was behind this, and Matt was sure he was, then Alex was in a very real danger.

Then he remembered the old steamer. It was a long shot but he had looked everywhere else. He raced through the old city's streets toward the wharf. He called out for help as he passed the *Amazing Grace* and frantically ran down the pier toward Simson's steamer as a scream split the air.

Alex?

He rushed forward, hoping he wasn't too late. The screams made him push himself harder. Sweat beaded along his brow as fast as it fell in streams down his face. As he reached the steamer, he noticed a thin trail of smoke drifting from the lower decks.

Just as he was about to push through the double doors leading onto the main deck, a glint of gold caught his eye. His chest heaving from exertion, he stooped down and picked up the golden heart that Alex's father had given her and shoved it in his pocket.

"Alex?" he screamed.

The smell of smoke was intense, and he heard the sharp crackling of burning wood under his feet as he rushed through the doors and into the old steamboat.

As he hurried toward the source of the fire, he nearly tumbled down the flight of stairs leading to the galley when he saw Jonah leaning against the wall. When the young man saw him, he jumped back, his eyes wide with fright.

The knowledge hit Matt all at once with a force so powerful it stole his breath. The hogs' poisoning, their release, Alex's fall into the river . . . Jonah had been at the center of it all. Betrayal knifed through him.

"Where is she?" he demanded, lifting Jonah up by his shirt.

"G-galley."

Matt eyed the young boy whom he had taken under his wing. There was nothing he could do to punish him now. Alex needed him.

Jonah held out his hand. On his palm, a key rested. Matt grabbed it and rushed down the stairs towards the galley, but was pushed back by a wall of flames. The key was useless since he couldn't reach the door.

He raced through the boat, trying to find another way down to the galley. Pausing to catch his breath, he sank to his knees in the abandoned dining room.

"Nooooo!" he shouted. He wouldn't lose her. He needed her. She was everything to him.

The fire crackled in the walls, seeming to mock him. Standing, a handle caught his eye. Remembering Lou, he thought it would work. It had to work. It might be Alex's only chance.

Simson knocked twice on the door, two short raps, apparently Jonah's signal. It was now or never, Alex thought. She jumped to her feet, running at him full force. Shoving him from behind, she pushed his head into the door.

Black smoke filled the room, making it harder to see.

Simson stumbled, raising his stick, and she didn't hesitate to kick him in his shin. He doubled over and she kneed him in the stomach, giving silent thanks to her father who taught her how to defend herself. She jumped out of the way as he crashed to the ground.

Coughing as the smoke became thicker, she covered her nose and mouth with the hem of her shirt. Where was Jonah? Why wasn't he opening the door? She copied Simson's knock, but again, nothing happened.

Smoke burned her eyes. Flames crawled up the wall and across the ceiling. Perspiration snaked down her cheeks. A crack sounded and she watched in heightened horror as pieces of the ceiling collapsed in around her.

Keeping her shirt's hem over her mouth and nose, she tried taking only shallow breaths. She was getting dizzy, imagining that she heard her name.

It was a whisper and she wondered if it was God calling her home. No, she thought in a stupor, it wouldn't be God. Because she hadn't confessed her sins, heaven wouldn't be her final destination. She whispered a quick prayer of absolution, hoping it would be enough, at least, to get her to Purgatory.

Then she heard it again—her name as quiet as a soft breeze. The flames lapped her feet and she backed against the only wall not engulfed. There she heard her name again. Louder now than before.

Again and again. Was she imagining it, or was someone actually calling her name? Shuffling to her feet, she tried to follow the noise.

"Alex? Are you down there?"

Matthew. It was Matthew's voice! She clawed at the wall. His voice was coming from behind it, she was sure of it.

She opened her mouth to call his name, but no words emerged, only squeaks.

Frantically she ran her hands over the wall. Clawing, fighting.

Another chunk of ceiling fell behind her and she jumped to her left, pressing her back against the wall. Wincing in pain as a piece of metal dug into her back, she turned around, trying to figure out what she had bumped into. It was a handle of some kind.

She pushed and pulled, and finally, out of desperation yanked downward. A door popped out of the wall.

The smoke hampered her vision, but she could make out a box.

"Alex!"

Relief flooded her. Matthew's voice was louder now as it floated down to her.

"M—Matth—" She coughed, her lungs burning.

"Alex!"

She heard the relief in his voice.

"Get in the dumbwaiter!"

The dumbwaiter! A way out! Using her hands, she felt for the shelves and quickly removed them all. She hoisted herself into the box, drawing her knees to her chin.

"That's a girl!"

Tears coursed down her face. She would be okay. Matthew was here. She would be okay.

The dumbwaiter jerked upward. Stopped. Jerked upward. Stopped. It seemed to her that the smoke chased her up the shaft. Just when she thought she would faint from fear and exhaustion, strong arms pulled her from the box. Her legs buckled beneath her and her eyes widened as she was swept into Matthew's arms.

"We need to get off," he yelled.

The fire blazed around them, easily igniting the old steamboat's wooden structure. It raged around them and Alex sank her head into Matthew's chest to protect her face from the flames.

A wail stopped them: "Kinkade."

Simson. They looked at each other for the briefest of seconds, then Matthew lowered the dumbwaiter to the galley. It took both their strength to pull the dumbwaiter upward, but finally Simson climbed out of it, coughing and choking and covered with soot.

Matthew ushered her through the thick smoke, away from the flames, leaving Simson to follow behind, left on his own.

The first gulps of fresh air hurt to breathe in, but felt heavenly. Matthew grabbed onto her arm. "We have to jump, sweet."

Darting a glance at the water, twenty feet below them if a foot, she shook her head, sooty curls tumbling over her eyes.

"I don't have time to argue with you."

She tightened her grip on the railing as he pried her fingers from the old iron. Too weak, she was no match for him. He swooped her into his arms and pitched her into the dirty river.

The fall over the railing felt like one in a dream. Surreal, floating, almost as though she were flying. Then she hit the water, plunging downward into darkness. Flailing, she looked up and saw the light of day above the surface. Slowly, she rose to the surface, gasping for breath.

No sooner had her head emerged than did Matthew clamp his forearm over her chest and pulled her weight on top of his. With sure kicks, he tugged her away from the burning boat and toward the pier. Somewhere near, she could hear Simson splashing as he made his way toward the dock.

Chill seeped into her bones, and she shivered helplessly as Matthew towed her toward safety, all the while rambling about swimming lessons under his breath. Looking up at the wharf, she could see dozens of people milling about. Fire volunteers were watching helplessly, knowing there was nothing they could do to save the engulfed steamboat. A rope ladder appeared from above, and Matthew heaved her up. Reaching out, she grabbed a sodden rung.

Her clothes seemed as though they weighed a hundred pounds, but somehow she managed to climb the swaying ladder. As she neared the top, several hands reached out and pulled her onto the wharf where she was immediately covered in blankets.

Someone settled her on the ground. Her teeth chattered and the next few minutes were a blur as a doctor listened to her breathing and pronounced her well enough not to go to a hospital and left her with strict orders to rest. Her voice, he said, would need a few days to heal.

She watched as Simson was first treated by doctors on hand, then taken away, along with Jonah, by policemen. She looked away as they were loaded into a locked wagon. Her gaze sought her husband.

Matthew looked like a drowned rag doll, she mused. His hair was slick, dripping onto his cheeks, down his back. His suit, she saw, was soaked. He scowled as the doctor examining him continued to pepper him with questions.

Suddenly he looked up, caught her gaze. In his eyes she saw his fear, his relief. His love for her. Slowly, he rose to his feet, brushing away the doctor trying to listen to his lungs.

Their gazes locked as they moved slowly toward one another, until Alex could take no more. Dropping her blanket, she ran to him. He held his arms open wide and she pressed herself into his embrace, feeling safe. Loved.

He smelled rotten, looked even worse, and she imagined she looked no better. And oh, how she loved him.

She rested her head on his shoulder as he guided her through throngs of onlookers. She peeked over her shoulder. The steamboat had disappeared beneath the water, only the tip of its hull remaining above the waterline. The memories of what happened aboard that steamer were fresh, and she had a feeling that they would stay with her for a long time to come. But they didn't matter now. All that mattered was that she was alive. Matthew was alive. Her family was safe. She was grateful.

"I—"

"Shh," he whispered. "The doctor said no talking. The burns to your throat need time to heal."

I love you, she wanted to say. To shout, for all the world to hear.

"Iloveyou," she said quickly, her voice hoarse, unrecognizable. She wondered if he even understood her.

"I told you no talking. Insufferable," he said in a teasing tone, shaking his head.

She frowned.

For a brief moment he let her go. After reaching in his pocket, he said, "I have something that belongs to you." He held up her pendant, and tears gathered in her eyes.

"You told me that your father gave this to you as a remembrance that your heart first belonged him. Well," he said with great emotion as he placed the broken chain into her open palm. "I give it back to you knowing that your heart now belongs to me, too, where I will keep it, tucked safe and secure next to mine forever. I love you, too, Alex. Always have. Always will. I told you before that I wasn't going to let you go. Not even a burning boat will stop me. Did you think I'd let you get away so easily?"

"Mat—"

"Shhh!" Pressing a finger to her lips.

Unable to speak the great welling of emotion she felt, she launched herself into his arms, knocking both of them down in the process.

His laughter washed over her as he sat up, never leaving her embrace.

Matt ran a hand through his hair. "As much as I hate to admit it, the days of steamboats are coming to an end. Railroads are simply too easy, too fast, and too cheap a competition. Soon there will be railroads connecting every city, railroad bridges crossing every river. There will be no need for steamers at all."

"I refuse to believe that," Lou said adamantly. She perched prettily on the edge of his desk. "People love steamboats. They're more than just transportation. They're romantic and mystical, and lazy . . . and fun," she added.

"Exactly," Matt agreed.

"You're confusing me," Jack said, tipping up her cowboy hat.

"And also me," Cal added. "I'm not even sure why I'm here. Isn't this a family meeting?"

"You are family," Alex pointed out in a scratchy voice.

Matt looked at her, cozied up on the couch, a blanket tucked around her. She was healing. Slowly, but surely. However, he, better than anyone, knew the wounds not visible to the eye were the hardest to heal. She'd had a tough time sleeping this past week, and he hoped her fears would soon ebb with the tide.

"W-why," Cal stammered. "Thank you."

She smiled, as did her sisters. They were quite a family, Matt reflected. His family. He laughed to himself. His and Cal's.

His gaze sought his wife's again as Lou teased Cal about becoming a Parker. Alex had taken the news of their home being sold better than he would have thought. There was a depth of sadness in her eyes that hadn't been there before he told her about the auction, and he had to wonder how long the shadow would last.

Finally, the conversation in the room turned back to the *Amazing Grace's* fate.

Alex stood, took his hand, and cleared her throat. "We're saying that we wish to make the *Amazing Grace* into a steamboat that doesn't carry cargo at all. We'll focus on the passengers. We'll reopen the ballroom, have theater performances—"

"A showboat?" Lou said doubtfully.

"Not quite," Matt said. "The East Coast spas are generating a lot of attention these days; a luxurious place for the whole family to spend their vacation."

"You want to turn the *Amazing Grace* into a resort?" Jack asked, incredulous.

"Of a sort," Matt answered. "It's clear that if we keep shipping cargo, we'll be out of business in a few years. Sad, but true. We need to change with the times. We'll turn the boat into a floating hotel. A place where families can come for relaxation. Couples can take wedding trips. We'll turn it into the finest hotel in these parts."

Jack sat in his chair behind the desk. Matt couldn't help but notice the way she kept looking at Cal. Maybe someday . . . "We have no money," she said. "How are we going to make the *Amazing Grace* a floating palace?"

Alex said, "We'll use the profits we make from this trip, and after repaying Cal's generosity, Matthew is going to invest the insurance money from the *Muddy Waters* into the *Amazing Grace*'s transformation, plus," she said wistfully, "the money we were going to use on the house."

"There will be dancing, singing, games . . . ," Matt listed.

Alex added, "There will be a dress shop and a salon for the women."

"What about the men?" Lou asked.

Matt smiled at Jack. "Any ideas?"

A smile blossomed, growing wider as it reached her eyes. "A gaming room."

Matt nodded.

"With card tables, and dice games, and—"

"I knew the gaming room was a bad idea," Alex laughed.

"I can't wait to get started," Jack said, pushing back her chair. "I'm going to draw up some plans. Oh, I have so many ideas."

"Does that mean you're in favor?"

"Yes!"

"Lou?"

"Entertainment, you say?"

"Singing. Dancing. Plays."

Lou nodded, giving her consent. "I think it's a wonderful idea."

Matt pulled Alex into an embrace as Lou followed Jack from the room. "Looks like we're in business."

Epilogue

"You look lovely," Lou gushed.

"Thank you," Alex said, her eyes bright with pure joy.

"I hope you know I don't wear a dress for just anyone."

"I appreciate the gesture, Jack," Alex said, smiling. "It means a lot."

The carriage bounced over a rut and the three girls jostled in their seats. Slowly, the carriage pulled to a stop in front of the church.

"Are you nervous?" Lou asked.

"A bit. Not much. I feel anxious. Giddy. Almost as though I'm about to break out in spontaneous laughter."

"I'd like to see that," Jack teased, then sobered. "You haven't had much of it in your life."

Alex squeezed her hand. "I will now."

The driver opened the door and helped them out. Alex looked around. Crocuses had popped out of the ground, a harbinger of the spring to come. River Glen's only church looked different and it took Alex a moment to realize that it had been painted, a gleaming coat of bright white paint. It looked as though the siding had been repaired as well, and yes, there were no longer any cracks in the walkway.

Jack opened the door of the church, and Alex went in, followed by Lou.

"Hello," Alex called out.

"Shouldn't Matt be here?" Jack asked in a loud whisper.

"He and Cal will be here soon. Matthew mentioned that Cal had a message to be telegraphed back home."

"By any chance, do you know where his home is?" Jack queried, none too subtly.

Alex shook her head. "He's very tight-lipped about his family."

Jack sighed. "I know."

Alex pulled open the door of the church and stepped inside, noting that it too had changed. There were new pews, a new lectern, and the clear windows had been replaced with stained glass. For a brief moment she wondered whether she was in the right church.

"I thought I heard voices," a young man said, walking toward them.

"This is River Glen's parish, is it not?" Jack asked.

Apparently Jack was having doubts about their location as well.

"Oh yes," the stranger said. "Yes indeed."

He was a nice-looking man with warm blue eyes and a quick smile. He waited patiently as she and her sisters stared in amazement.

Alex came to her senses and offered her hand. "I'm Alex Kinkade. I sent a telegraph a week ago . . ." His brow furrowed. "To Reverend Pierson . . ."

"Ahhh, that explains it. The reverend retired nearly a

month ago. Left on immediate sabbatical. His mail is being forwarded to his new address. May I help you?"

Dismay worked its way into Alex's happy heart. This couldn't be happening. With the patience of a saint she had waited for this day. Each night while Matthew slept on the sofa in their stateroom, she had tried to lure him to the bed, without success, the infuriating man! He held fast in his beliefs to be married again before joining her in bed, and now it seemed as though she would have to wait even longer.

"I hope so," she stammered, a blush heating her cheeks. "I'm to be married today. Well, remarried." At the man's quizzical look, she said, "It is a long story. Is it possible to be married today?" She hoped she didn't sound overly eager, though her sisters smiled openly at her discomfiture.

"Today?" the man said.

"Has the parish found a replacement for Reverend Pierson yet?" Alex asked.

The man's quick smile was back. "You're looking at him. I'm John Hewitt. Reverend John Hewitt."

Alex's eyes widened in shock. He was so young! "Oh. I'm so sorry; I didn't realize. Reverend Hewitt, these are my sisters, Jack Parker. . . ."

His eyes sparkled. "Ahhh, the famous Parker sisters. I've heard much about you," he said, taking Jack's offered hand.

Alex was sure she didn't want to know what the townsfolk had been saying, so she didn't dwell on it. "And this is my other sister, Lou Parker," she finished.

Alex watched with growing interest as Lou and the reverend seemed to be at a loss for words. She caught Jack's gaze over Lou's head and smiled. Jack sighed and shook her head.

"Charmed." The reverend took Lou's hand, held it tight.

"It's nice to meet you, Reverend Hewitt," Lou said, shyly.

"I have been wanting to thank you all," he said, surprising them.

"Why?" Alex asked. "What have we done for you?"

"For taking such wonderful care of your home. I love living there."

"You bought our house?" Jack said in a rush.

"I did, and I love it. It's wonderfully warm and inviting. "Odd," he said, "but sometimes I could swear I hear the laughter of small girls in the hallways."

Somehow the knowledge relieved Alex. To know that this man would appreciate her home, and would undoubtedly fill it with children made her smile. She again noticed the way Lou and the reverend seemed to be so aware of one another. Her smile deepened.

"I'm glad the house is in such good hands."

The reverend returned her smile. "A wedding you said? I *am* available this afternoon, but does not a wedding require a groom these days?"

"I'm here," a deep, familiar voice said from behind them.

Matthew and Cal came down the small center aisle. Alex's breath caught as she looked at her husband, her groom. He stepped forward and took her hand in his. It was strong, warm. He smelled like soap, fresh and clean. Never in her wildest fantasies did she believe she could ever be this happy.

He leaned in and kissed her. "You look so beautiful."

The reverend coughed. "I believe that is to be saved for after the ceremony." His grin was quick. "It will take me a moment to prepare things."

Alex blushed deeply, heat staining her cheeks. Matthew

took her arm and led her up the aisle, Lou, Jack, and Cal falling in behind them.

"To love and to cherish," he whispered, running his fingers through the loose curls hanging freely down her back.

She stopped in front of the lectern. Gazing up into his eyes, she murmured, "To comfort and keep you."

On a whisper, he added, "To honor and obey."

"We'll work on that one," she said, laughing.

He cupped her face, brought his lips close to hers, barely touching, barely breathing. Then he smiled. "Insufferable."